THE NARROW GATE (SOLOM #2)

Scott Nicholson

Copyright ©2014 Scott Nicholson
Haunted Computer Books

ISBN: 978-1-62647-069-9

Haunted Computer Books
P.O. Box 135
Todd, NC 28684 USA

CHAPTER ONE

The Blackburn River was as old as its secrets.

Geologists said it was one of the oldest rivers in the world, erupting up and cutting through the Appalachian Mountains when those ancient peaks were still young and jagged.

The people in Solom didn't care about history books. All they saw was the slim ribbon of silver that cut into the granite below the brown banks of the hilltops. The water brought sustenance in the spring, kept their stock alive in the summer, and in September it shot its narrow currents among the yellow and white stones. It slowed to a trickle in January, only to bust out white again during the March melt. The water, like the humans who clustered around its shores, moved with the tug of forces beyond their understanding.

The community of Solom took its name from bad grammar. Some say the place used to be called Solomon Branch, after the Old Testament king. Others said it was Solomn, a misspelling of the word "solemn," which meant everything from formal and serious in a liturgical sense to grave and somber, as in a funeral ceremony. The permanent valley settlers had eventually trimmed off the silent letter at the end, most never even realizing it was there. If it sounded like Solom, then it was Solom.

The original residents were the buffalo that trampled ruts across the hilltops as they made their way from Kentucky in the summer to the Piedmont flatlands of North Carolina in the winter. The herds numbered in the thousands, and the ground shook as their hooves bit into the earth. The Cherokee and

Catawba visited the region only in the fall, when meat was available. Otherwise, the natives had the good sense to stay off those cold and forlorn mountaintops. Then the whites came along and poured across the slopes like albino fire ants on a brown sugar hill.

Daniel Boone and the early European trappers and hunters were cold-natured enough to hang out on the trails and slaughter their quarry across the seasons, with no sense of a circular food chain. In a few short decades, the buffalo and elk that sustained the natives for centuries were gone, remembered only in the occasional place name or flea-ridden floor skin.

The Cherokee endured their own problems, driven at gunpoint to Oklahoma, where the landscape was as alien to them as if they had been dropped onto the surface of Mars. The federal government later felt guilty enough to grant them control of gambling casinos, but by then their heritage and souls had been all but lost. They dreamed of spiritual journeys where they met up with buffalo, but they woke up to a modern world that encouraged hatred in every sector of society, especially against the outcast.

Not that modern Solom paid any attention. The inhabitants were mostly the offspring of farm and lumber workers, the women thick and faithful, the men prone to drink when they weren't in church. All were raised with a sense of duty, and church records were often the final statement on the quality of a life lived.

A man's obituary was set down by a barely literate family member, and if the man lived a good life, he was noted as a solid provider, a friend of the church and community, and an honest trader. If he failed in any of those areas, his obituary was nothing more than an opportunity to question the eventual resting place of his soul.

Women were measured within a narrower yet more sophisticated set of parameters. Were her hips broad enough to bear a goodly number of children? Did she sit quietly on her side of church, raising her voice only at the appropriate time, after the males established the proper cadence? Did she keep the Bible on her lap instead of the shelf? Did her obituary list more than a dozen grandchildren?

But Solom's most notorious resident made such boundaries seem foolish. No obit had ever been written for Harmon Smith, and his name was marked in no family Bible.

Many testimonials had been recorded about the work of Good Harmon Smith, a Methodist minister who crossed denominational lines in the late 1800s, whose horse Old Saint touched half of three states. A rival minister, the Rev. Duncan Blackburn, attended to the needs of Episcopalians and the few mountain Catholics. Blackburn earned a resting place on holy ground while Smith died on the slopes of what became known as Lost Ridge.

The public records said Smith was on his way to a January bedside appointment with a dying widow when a blizzard swept down from Canadian tundra and paid his holy debt in full. In the twenty-first century, Duncan Blackburn was featured in a line-drawing portrait buried in the back pages of a university library book while Harmon Smith occupied graves in three different churchyards. No one knew where Smith's real remains were buried, but each of the congregations hoped it wasn't their own sacred ground that had been sullied.

And some questioned if there were any remains left worth returning to the dirt.

But this was Solom, home of an old river, and questions only came from those who didn't know any better. From outsiders, and newcomers, and those who heard the soft sound of distant twilight hoof beats.

Duncan Blackburn was history, but Harmon Smith still lived. Whenever a branch rustled in the dark forest, whenever a barn door made a slow sweep on rusty hinges, whenever an old woman needed to scare a wayward child into proper behavior, then Harmon Smith's name was invoked. As a dead man, he'd gathered a much larger flock than he had during his days as a horseback preacher.

And on this October night, it was time to ride again.

CHAPTER TWO

It was seven minutes before his return when Sarah Jeffers ran her broom along the baseboard of the counter.

Mouse doodie.

The counter stood by the front door of Solom General Store and was dark maple, the top scarred by two million transactions. Most of the lights were turned off for closing time, and the dolls, tools, mountain crafts, and just plain junk that hung from the ceiling beams threw long shadows against the walls. After all her years as proprietor, the aroma of tobacco, woodstove smoke, licorice, and shoe polish had seeped into her skin like water.

The store was built during the town's heyday just before World War I, when the timber industry made its assault on the local hardwoods. The train station had been a bustling place, bringing Sarah's grandparents to the mountains from Pennsylvania. The Jeffers, who had once gone by the family name of Jaffe, built the store from the ground up, collecting the creek stones for the foundation, trading and bartering for stock, even breeding their own work force. They were Jewish but no one paid that any mind, because they kept closed services in their living room and the store remained open on both Saturdays and Sundays.

When the forest slopes were nothing but stumps and the timber cutters moved on, the sawmill shut down. After that, it was like the hands ran backwards on the clock. The earthen dam slowly eroded on Blackburn River, and the little housing settlement that sprang up around the mill began succumbing to the gray and ceaseless weight of gravity. Though the first Fords made occasional visits over the dusty mountain roads, mostly driven by lumber barons who wanted to check on their investments, the town's slow exodus was almost entirely via horse-and-wagon. By the Great Depression, Solom was little more than a whistle stop on the Virginia Creeper railroad line. Then came the great 1940 flood, sweeping away the station and a third of the remaining houses, killing a dozen people in the process.

Sarah's grandparents died within weeks of one another, and the three children fought over who should stay and run the store. The short straw belonged to Sarah's father Elisha, who promptly took on a Primitive Baptist wife, Laurel Lee, because she knew addition and subtraction and silence. Through it all the general store stood on its little rise above the river, the stock changing with the times. Chesterfield tobacco pouches and Bugler papers gave way to Marlboro tailor-mades, horehound stick candy disappeared from the shelves in favor of Baby Ruth bars. A Sears & Roebuck catalog by the register once allowed a mountain family to order practically anything a New York city slicker could buy, but that had been replaced by a computer during the Clinton era. Sarah didn't trust it, even naming it "Slick Willy" and suspected it of swallowing a dollar once in a while, and the screen stayed black unless Greta, the thick-ankled college student who worked part-time, was on the clock.

The computer was one of the few modern touches, besides the sheer volume of cheap imported crafts designed to look folksy. The wall adornments—rusty advertising signs, farm implements, and shelves of old ripple glass bottles—furthered the illusion that the general store was lost in a time, a nostalgic reminder of more carefree days. Sarah didn't buy the illusion, but she sold it. Times were better raking in leisure dollars rather than dunning the local folks for nickels.

Sarah had grown up in the store, dusting the shelves and tallying pickled eggs in her plain cotton shift. She remembered when the store's first indoor toilet was installed, and though as a four-year-old she'd suffered a great fear of the roaring flush of water, she'd had an even greater fear of hanging her bare bottom over that stinky black hole in the outhouse. Even back then, she'd pushed a broom, and she asked her mother about the numerous little black needles amid the stray hair, spilled sugar, dried grass, and dirt.

"Mouse doodie," Laurel Lee Jeffers said. "A mouse goes to heaven in a country store."

Sarah always thought of those mice as happy, blessed creatures, scurrying under the floorboards, worrying their way through sacks of feed grain, chewing into the corners of cornflake boxes. But after nearly seventy years of sweeping up their damned doodie, she was about ready to wish them to a Baptist hell.

But at least the mice gave her something to blame when strange sounds echoed through the aisles. She didn't like being in the store alone, but she could barely afford her two part-time helpers. So she'd spent the past decades running the broom, ignoring the evidence of her ears, and not thinking about the Horseback Preacher, the Scarecrow Man, and all the other tales her mother told her.

The bell over the screen door rang. It was ten minutes after seven, past closing time, but she hadn't locked the door. The porch light bathed the deck in yellow light, and Sarah squinted against it at the bulky shadow.

"Howdy," she said. It was still tourist season in the mountains, although the Floridians and New Yorkers were usually tucked away in their Titusville hotel rooms by now, afraid of getting a mosquito bite, or else squirreled away in their Happy Hollow rental cabins at $150 a night. The kayak and rafting trade from Sue Norwood's little shop had boomed along the river, helping the general store keep its head above water. Seemed like every time the business wanted to sink down to the sandy bottom and take a nice, long nap, some money-making scheme came along and dragged it back to the surface for another gasp. Usually the scheme relied on outsiders, because there wasn't enough cash in Solom to stock the old outhouse with paper.

The shadow stood in the door, hands in pockets, the head obscured by an outdated hat with a wide brim. All Sarah wanted was to get a little of his money and send him on his way in time for the latest rerun of "Seinfeld," delivered via her little satellite dish.

"Can I get you something?" she asked, glad to be shut of mouse doodie for the moment. Her family's cultured diction had given way to a mountain twang over the years, partly unconsciously and partly to help sell the down-home illusion.

The figure shuffled forward. People in these parts, even the visitors, usually answered when addressed. But occasionally a creep came through looking for the best place in the neighborhood for fast money. She did a mental calculation, figured the register held maybe eighty bucks. Worth killing somebody over, these days.

Sarah leaned her broom against the counter, flicking her eyes toward the shotgun she kept on the second shelf beneath the register. The shotgun was well-oiled but hadn't been fired in twenty years. Currently it was covered by stacks of the High Country News, a free weekly that was such wretched oatmeal she couldn't give it away. She'd hidden the newspapers, not wanting to disappoint the friendly young man with the crewcut who delivered them early Thursday mornings. She figured there was at least two months of bad copy between her and the firearm.

She'd have to talk her way out of this one. "Got a special on canned ham," she said. "Nine dollars. Let the missus take an evening off from the kitchen."

Nothing, not even a grunt. The man was three steps inside. She wished she'd left more lights on. It was the electrical cooperative's fault. In her father's day, the Blackburn dam ran a generator, cranking out enough juice to light up the store and two dozen homes. Then the co-op came in and hooked five counties together, and you were either on the grid or off, no in between. After that, the power bill had gotten higher every month.

Sarah could make out the man's form now, the collar of his coat turned up even though the fall had yet to turn chilly. The front brim of the hat was angled down, keeping the face in shadows.

The stranger stood there, his breath like the whistle of a distant train. Something creaked in the hardware section, in the back corner of the store that Sarah avoided after sundown. Things went wrong in that corner: alkaline batteries leaked, boxes of nails busted open for no good reason, the fingers of work gloves somehow grew holes.

Her father sold guns, and the ammunition used to be locked away in that corner, but one afternoon some of the bullets somehow got hot and exploded, sending lead fragments whizzing over the heads of the customers. Sarah wished for a magic bullet right now, one that would knock the stranger's hat off his head.

Because the hat didn't belong.

"Your first trip to Solom?" Sarah said, keeping her voice steady. She eased toward the counter, closer to the register and the shotgun. She'd been driving some tacks into the shelf so she could hang her metal signs, the ones that said "A Bad

Day of Fishing Beats a Good Day of Work" and "I Ain't Old, I'm Just Experienced." She leaned on the counter with one elbow, her other arm reaching for the claw hammer. It felt good in her hand.

"You staying up at the Tester B & B?" she asked the mute man. "Or the Happy Hollow cabins?"

Sarah brought the hammer closer to her hip, imagining its arc as she brought it into the dark, unseen face. Her lips creased into the tired, welcoming smile she gave to first-time customers, an expression meant to elicit pity and a desire to help out a little old lady through the kindness of a loose wallet. "You ain't from around here, are you?"

The stranger stepped into the light, lifted his hat, and smiled. "Once I was," he said, in a voice as patient as a river and as deep as Satan's driest well. "But that was a while back."

Sarah dropped the hammer, nearly breaking her big toe.

CHAPTER THREE

"Not bad, Mom." Jett Draper crunched on the Banquet fried chicken, comforted by the salty crust that came from a factory batter-dipping process instead of a creepy old family recipe.

"Glad you like it," Katy Logan said. "How's school?"

"Boring."

"Only boring people get bored."

"Okay, then." Jett started to wipe the grease from her lips with a shirt sleeve, but Katy gave a pre-emptive glare of disapproval. "Made a B on my history test, started a new etching in Art, and didn't see a single spooky scarecrow or dead preacher."

"Jett, please." Katy stood and began clearing the table, obviously dodging the issue yet again. A year had passed since Gordon Smith freaked out and attacked the both of them, as well as Jett's dad, and besides the statement she'd been forced to give to the police after Gordon's death, she'd barely mentioned it.

In some ways, she was just as much of a Stepford Mom now as she was back then, Jett thought.

All of them lied about what really happened. According to the official police report, Gordon attacked her dad in a jealous rage and was killed in an act of self-defense. Even though the Smith family had lived in the area for generations, he was enough of an oddball that nobody was surprised that he'd launched into a murderous rampage. Jett could still hear the whispers in the high school hallways and cold eyes followed them down the aisles of the old general store, but Jett made the most of her newfound celebrity.

She'd amped up her Goth act even more, with black, thick-soled Doc Martens and a few extra chains on her leather jacket. The three piercings in her left ear might not have stood out in the big city, but in Solom they gave a clear signal that Jett most emphatically wasn't a native. A streak of bright blue ran down one side of her dark hair, and Mom finally relented and let her wear eye shadow and lipstick. Three years away from college, she was fully prepared to push the buttons of the hillbillies and farm boys and the occasional stuck-up tourist who rolled though the valley to look at the colorful autumn foliage.

"Is that still one of those things we don't talk about?" Jett taunted. "So your husband tried to kill you. Big deal. Happens all the time."

"I'm past that," Katy said, standing at the sink with her back turned to Jett.

"Are you past the part where we were saved by a supernatural preacher from hell?"

Katy let the dishes clank together. "I'd rather not talk about it."

"Come on, Mom. You were rocking it that night."

"I'm just glad we got through it together. Come on, we've got to feed the goats."

Jett wished Mom sold all the goats, but because Gordon hadn't left a will, her attorney advised her to keep all the property together until a civil court adjudicated the case. One of Gordon's cousins, Charlie Smith, had filed a claim on the property and threatened a civil suit for wrongful death. Katy's strategy was to just wait him out and allow the passage of time to weaken his position. That meant she couldn't sell the property, and since she only earned part-time income as an accountant, they couldn't afford to move or rent another place.

Like she will ever let me forget that it's my fault we're stuck here. Talk about your guilt trips.

"Can't we just let the furry little buttheads eat each other?" Jett asked.

"They've mellowed out a lot since then. I'm starting to like them."

"Mom!"

Katy turned around and grinned. Jett suspected her mom was just trying to change the subject, but she was right: the goats were actually kind of neat now that they weren't trying to drag them down and devour the flesh from their bones. In a way, Jett could even relate to them. Like her, they were quirky, stubborn, and hard to keep penned in.

"I'm changing out of my good boots first," Jett said, heading for the stairs. "Don't want to get any goat poop on them."

Mom redecorated after Gordon's death, and there was little sign of the university professor who obsessed over obscure Appalachian religions. The leather-bound books were packed away in the attic, along with his collection of sacred relics, folk art, and tobacco pipes. Mom had yet to add her own touch, so the interior still screamed "ancient, dusty farmhouse that might be haunted." Jett was sure that *oeuvre* had its own category in *Better Homes & Gardens*.

Jett didn't want to think about ghosts, especially the headless ghost of Gordon's first wife. Jett suspected the spirit may have possessed Mom for a while there, which seemed to have turned her into Stepford Mom, happy being a brainless housewife with a fondness for recipes. As with the sinister, cheese-faced preacher, the ghost seemed to have vanished the night Gordon died.

Maybe that's why Mom wants to forget. If you don't think about it, it's easy to believe it never happened. Except for Gordon's grave at Free Will Baptist.

As she clumped up the stairs, she fished her cell phone out of her jacket pocket. It didn't get any decent signals on the farm unless she was in the barn loft, but sometimes texts managed to leak through. Bethany Miller, the closest thing to a best friend, invited her to go see a James Bond movie, ending with "DD with Tommy?" That was a joke. Tommy Wilson had once been Jett's drug dealer, but she'd been off the stuff—and away from Tommy—for more than year. No way were they going on a double date with Bethany and her stud boyfriend Chuck.

After deleting that one, a message from Dad popped up: "Still on for Monday?"

Sure, Dad. Wouldn't miss it for the world.

Dad had been clean and sober for a year, too, although they didn't talk much about it. While Jett's problem was mostly marijuana, Dad sampled the buffet of everything from cocaine to liquor, and his prior drug arrest had drawn the attention of local law enforcement—if not for the vicious gashes Gordon inflicted with his scythe, Dad would likely have been charged with manslaughter if not murder.

As it was, nobody quite considered him a hero, but he'd started up a construction business and settled in Solom. Jett was kind of glad to have him around, even though Mom insisted there wasn't a chance in hell the two of them would ever reconcile their divorce.

Jett entered a message "*YOLO. C U THERE.*"

She wasn't prone to childish Internet shorthand but its use never failed to irk Dad a little, and she always got a giggle when he asked for a translation. Just before entering her room, she glanced at the closet that contained the access door to the attic.

If you're around, Rebecca, please stay up there.

She quickly changed into her skuzzy sneakers and a ratty flannel shirt, making the transition from Goth princess to Ruby Jean Redneck in less than a minute. After Gordon's death, she'd not felt the need to be so visibly defiant at home, so she'd replaced the band posters on her wall with photo-shopped fantasy landscapes featuring mist-wreathed cliffs, lush vegetation, and spectacular creatures like soaring dragons and winged unicorns. It clashed a little with her adopted fashion style, and she would be horrified if any of her classmates visited, but the contradictions were part of some inner transformation that she only vaguely sensed was taking place.

She glanced out the window, where sunset limned the mountain ridges with golden lava that was as surreal as anything in her posters. The barn stood in dark silhouette, and beyond it was the little patch of garden she and Mom tended through the summer. No scarecrow, thank God. If the birds wanted to eat, let them.

She hurried downstairs and Mom was waiting by the door with a flashlight and hardwood walking stick.

"Let's do this," Jett said, taking the walking stick from her. The weapon was a nod to past horrors, but the ritual of "feeding the goats" was fueled by their determination not to let fear run their lives. Mom was convinced that Gordon's death satisfied whatever evil force the man had summoned. Jett wasn't so sure, since the legends of the Horseback Preacher and the Scarecrow Man had apparently been floating around Solom long before Jett and Katy had arrived.

Probably even before the dinosaurs. Solom was just that weird.

"Maybe we should hire Odus Hampton to do this," Jett said as they descended the porch steps. "He knows his way around the farm."

"You know I can't afford that. Besides, we're like one big, happy family now."

"It would be a bigger family with Dad around."

"That's not cool, Jett. You can't live in the past."

"There's no way he was a worse husband than Gordon. Dad risked his life to save us, remember?"

"It's complicated. Someday, when you're grown up, you'll understand."

"Sure," Jett said, waving the stick to indicate the Smith homestead that Katy inherited. "It all makes perfect sense. Gordon was into some kind of freaky harvest-religion trip and he wanted to chop us up to appease some ancient backwoods god or another. But the Horseback Preacher didn't want any competition, so he showed up and kicked ass."

"You can't live in the past."

"But you can almost *die* there."

Mom opened the gate to the pasture. The barn was a hundred feet away from the barbed-wire fence. Dusk deepened, and the barn stood like a warped, wooden cathedral that demanded rites best performed away from human eyes.

"Maybe we should feed them before it gets dark, huh?" Jett whispered.

"Got to keep the family happy, right?"

"Or else," Jett said, sliding the barn door open. The tribe of goats bleated in hunger as they stepped inside.

CHAPTER FOUR

Arvel Ward drew the curtains and turned away from the window.

"Anything out there, honey?" his wife Betsy asked.

"Nothing worth talking about."

They'd reached that point of marriage where there wasn't a whole lot of *anything* worth talking about. That was just fine with Arvel. Talking sometimes stirred up feelings. Betsy might get in the mood for a romantic walk in the moonlight, and that wouldn't do.

Nights like this were best spent indoors. Goats would be walking tonight, and him that held sway over them. Other things would be afoot, too. Autumn was a time of bad magic. Solom didn't need a Halloween midnight to open the door between the living and the dead; the door was already as thin as the gilt-edged pages of a dry Bible, and about as easy to punch through.

Arvel had first seen Harmon Smith, better known as the Horseback Preacher, on a pig path on the back side of Lost Ridge. Arvel was nine years old and on his way back from a Rush Branch fishing hole when he stopped at a gooseberry thicket. It was August, and the berries were fat and pink, with green tiger stripes. Gooseberries gave him the runs, so he knew better than to keep eating them, but they were so tangy sweet he couldn't stop shoveling them in his mouth, despite the three rainbow trout in the little reed basket he used for a creel.

Harmon came upon him while Arvel was lying in the

shade, his belly swole up like a tick's. Arvel squinted as the man stood with his back to the sun, the face lost in the wide, worn brim of the rounded hat. Arvel knew who it was right off. The Horseback Preacher walked the hills looking for his horse, and had been looking ever since those other preachers pitched in and murdered him. Arvel couldn't rightly blame Harmon Smith for doing all the terrible things people said he did. After all, he was buried in three different graves and that wasn't any way for a soul to find peace, especially for a man of the cloth.

Legend had it Harmon pitched Johnny Hampton under the water wheel at the old Rominger grist mill, and Johnny's foot got caught in one of the paddles. Over and over went little Johnny, shouting and blubbering each time his head broke free of the water, grabbing a lungful of air just before he went under again. Took about twenty rounds before he tuckered out and drowned, while the mill hands desperately tried to stop the wheel. His death went down in the church records and the county deed office as an accident, but folks in Solom kept their own secret ledger.

Arvel's great-uncle Kenny was galloping down a moonlit road when he came to the covered bridge that used to cross the river near the general store. Everybody liked the nice echo of horseshoes clanging off those wooden runners, so Kenny picked up speed and burst through. Trouble was, a carpenter had been doing repairs on the bridge's roof that day and left a level line in the rafters. The line slipped during the night until it was about neck-high to a man on a horse. Kenny's head hadn't been cut clean through, but there was barely enough connecting meat left to stuff a sausage casing.

Others had fallen into hay rakes, caught blood poisoning from saw blades, or got bitten by rattlesnakes. Old Willet Miller had been gored by a goat, his intestines yanked out and hanging like noodles on a fork. So Arvel held no expectations of ever getting up and walking away from the encounter that long-ago day. He was just glad for two things: he'd go with a belly full of gooseberries and that he wouldn't have to clean the stinky, slimy fish before supper.

"Boy," Harmon Smith said in greeting, touching the brim of his hat. The voice held no fire and brimstone, not even the thunder of a preacher. It was just plain talk.

"You're the Horseback Preacher." Arvel figured it was no time for fooling around, plus he ought to be on his best behavior. Free Will Baptists earned their way to heaven, and Arvel figured he needed to do some making up for the horehound candy he'd pilfered from the jar down at the general store. Even stealing from a Jew probably counted as a sin in God's all-seeing eyes.

Harmon's head swiveled back and forth, offering just a hint of the man's angular nose and sharp chin. "Doesn't seem like I'm doing much riding, does it?"

Arvel squinted, trying to make out the man's eyes in that desperate black shadow beneath the hat. It almost seemed like the man had no face at all, only a solid glob of dark. His suit was black and pocked with holes, and he wore a tow-linen shirt, material only poor kids wore in those days. "You looking for your horse?"

"Why, have you seen one?"

Arvel made a big show of looking up and down the pig path. "I think I saw one down that way," he said, and nodded in the direction of the Ward farm.

Arvel couldn't have said the man exactly grinned, but the darkness broke in the lower part of the face, revealing a gleam of ochre enamel. "And I suppose you'd be leading me to it, right?"

"Why, yes, sir."

"Respect for elders. That speaks well for you, boy."

"I try to do right by people," Arvel said, as much for God's ears as for Harmon's.

"All right, show me that horse."

Arvel struggled to his feet, hitched up the suspenders he'd unhooked while digesting, and headed down the pig path, careful not to walk too fast. The Horseback Preacher followed, scuffed boots knocking dust in the air. Arvel tried to sneak a look back to catch the man's face now that they were heading into the sun, but somehow the preacher stayed just out of plain view. Arvel carried his cane pole over his shoulder, and wondered idly what would happen if his hook accidentally sunk in the Horseback Preacher's flesh. Could a dead man feel pain?

They went through the apple orchard that divided the Smith and Ward properties. The apples were small and tart, still weeks away from ripening, and Arvel's belly was already gurgling from all the gooseberries. He wondered if he'd have to make a dash behind a tree before they reached the outhouse. Would the Horseback Preacher give him privacy, or stand over him with the wooden door open while he did his business?

They came out of the trees and the Ward farm was spread out before them. Arvel's pappy was splitting wood by the house, and his brother Zeke was scattering seed corn for the chickens. Acres of hayfields surrounded them, and the crop garden was rich and green behind the house. There under the bright summer sun, Arvel felt safe.

"I don't see a horse," the Horseback Preacher said.

"Sure, it's there in the barn."

"You're lying to me, boy."

Arvel's heart was pumping like water from a spring hose. He threw aside his pole and the basket of fish and broke into a run, hollering and waving his arms. Despite the noise in his own head, the Horseback Preacher's voice came through clear from the shade of the orchard rows: "Liars go to the devil, boy. Know them by their fruits."

Pappy whipped him for raising a ruckus and startling the livestock, and Zeke snickered and teased for days afterward, but Arvel was fine with all that, because he was alive. Still, he knew Harmon Smith never forgot, and the ride never ended. Sooner or later, Arvel would have to own up to his lie.

He just hoped it wasn't tonight. Zeke was gone, but that was an accident, could have happened to anyone. Harmon Smith wasn't the type to wait for old age to claim Arvel. No, violence was his way. Harmon had been taken by violence and violence was what he delivered back to Solom.

"Talked to Gordon Smith's widow today," Betsy said, busy with her knitting.

"What did you tell her?"

"I kept my mouth shut. She's kind of standoffish."

"City folks. You know how they are."

"She probably thinks Gordon's death was the end of it," Betsy said. "Maybe I should have told them. That little girl of hers…"

"She ain't so little anymore. Flaunting around like some kind of floozy in all that make-up and them black clothes. Harmon Smith would strike her down in a heartbeat."

"Now, Arvel. It ain't our place to be casting no stones," Betsy said, coming dangerously close to challenging him. "We got along with the Smith family for years, even when everybody else steered clear of them."

"It's called being neighbors. You don't have to like it, but you got to live and let live."

"Until somebody dies, that is."

"Solom's restless," Arvel said, checking out the window

again. "He might be riding tonight."

"Should have warned her," Betsy said. "That would have been the Christian thing to do."

"Well, never hurts to mind your own business for a change."

"I did, honey. I minded it real hard."

Arvel locked the doors. Katy Logan and her tarted-up daughter would just have to take care of themselves. Neighbors were neighbors, but Solom was Solom.

And every fresh victim that stood between Arvel and the Horseback Preacher meant a longer wait until his own day of reckoning.

CHAPTER FIVE

Katy swept the flashlight beam around the barn.

Even though the sunset still cast its hellish glow, the interior of the old wooden structure offered little access to its rays. The barn had probably changed little in the decades since the Smiths built it, aside from a little leaning and warping of its planks and beams. The goats freely milled the pastures during the day, browsing on the scrub vegetation along the fence lines, but at night they sought shelter in their pens, waiting for their nightly feed.

Katy wasn't quite sure what would happen if the goats weren't sated, but an uneasy truce seemed preferable to the alternative. So she gave them extra grain and sweetened beet peels at bedtime, scooping the food from large metal trash cans secured in a corn crib. The goats knew the routine, so they crowded around Katy as she crossed the barn to the bin. She swallowed hard and tried to control her breathing. She was pretty sure they could sense fear, much the way a wild predator did.

Jett pulled an apple core from her pocket and waved it in the air to distract them. "Yo, Alfalfa Breath, over here."

Smelling the fruit, the goats immediately left Katy and closed around Jett, who then flung the bait onto the packed mud and loose straw of the barn floor. The goats butted heads and shoved one another in their frantic hunger. The chickens, drowsing in their nesting boxes, stirred and cooed.

"Go for it, Mom," Jett said, sitting on the loft steps so she didn't accidently get bumped by thrashing horns. The herd was down to eleven goats, and they'd ditched the creepy Old Testament names Gordon had given them in favor of movie-star names like Taylor, Channing, and Franco. They used the names interchangeably, though, with the exception of Dirty Harry, the big, bearded buck that was patriarch of the tribe.

Katy flipped the hasp on the corn crib, tucking the flashlight under her arm as she removed the lid from a trash can and scooped up some grain. Without looking, Katy flung the grain across the barn. The tribe scattered as each goat followed its keen nose to whatever delicate morsel lay nearby. Katy slung two heaping scoops in the long wooden trough and closed the crib.

"Good one, Mom, now let's get out of here," Jett said.

"We're not done yet."

"Do we have to?"

"You want to be able to sleep, don't you?"

Jett glanced up the loft stairs as if looking into an endless cave. "Okay, but you have to go first."

Katy veered around the goats and shined the flashlight along the barn walls and up to the loft door. Jett had encountered the Scarecrow Man up there, and even now she wasn't sure whether it was a supernatural creature or merely Gordon dressed up in his murdering costume. But it certainly was Gordon who attacked Mark up there with a scythe, and the blood still cast dark stains on some of the framework.

What the goats couldn't reach with their tongues, that is.

Katy grabbed the pitchfork—it was old habit by now—and let its tines lead her up the creaky steps. The goats bleated contentedly below, their musky smell filling the air. Jett followed with the walking stick. Jett visited the loft often during the day to use her cell phone and didn't take the routine as seriously anymore, thinking it boring, but Katy considered it an important part of their healing.

*You don't want to be jumping at shadows the rest of your life.
And neither do I.*

Katy pushed open the loft door with a groan of rusty
hinges. She swept the flashlight beam over the bales of hay
that Odus and Ray Tester had stacked there over the summer.
They'd made a deal with Ray to cut two of their pastures in
exchange for half the hay, and Ray paid Odus for helping.
Katy didn't want to drive a tractor, much less buy one, so the
arrangement worked out well. The store of hay was plenty
enough to get the goats through winter.

But hay wasn't the reason they were here. Katy waited
until Jett was in the loft and then she spotlighted the two
figures hanging from baling wire from the rafters. The first
was a limp stack of rags with a burlap sack face, features
crudely stitched. The fabric had ripped and brown cotton
leaked from the opening. A broad-brimmed straw hat was
perched atop the head, and dirty work gloves were sewn to
the ends of each flannel shirt sleeve. The faded jeans were tied
into thin, footless bundles at the end of each leg. Katy liked to
reassure herself that, even if the Smith family scarecrow
managed to free itself of the wire from which it hung, she'd
still be able to outrun it.

The second scarecrow was the one she'd originally found
inside a crate in the attic of the farmhouse. This one wore a
long linen dress and apron, clearly more feminine in its shape
than its counterpart. Even with the hay dust floating thick as
snuff, the odor of lilacs was piercing and sweetly distinct. This
scarecrow held its cheesecloth head in its "hands," a small red
smile stitched in the white fabric.

"See?" Katy said. "Still there."

"Why don't we just burn them?"

"It just feels...wrong. Here in the barn, we can keep track
of them. But if we can't see them, then we have no idea what

they're up to."

"And you have to face your fear or the fear wins. Blah blah blah."

"Hey, we're *winning* here. We've got the hang of this farm life, lots of fresh air and sunshine, organic produce and eggs, and a flock of goats that practically worship us."

"'Tribe,' Mom. A group of goats is called a 'tribe.' Sheep and chickens are flocks."

"Oh, right, Science Girl. Remind me why you're making a B in that class again?"

"To tick you off. Why else?" Jett tapped the walking stick against one of the empty wooden barrels. "No bodies in there. That's a good sign."

"Looks good to me. What say we head back to the house for some no-bake cookies?"

Jett gave her a look. "You don't want to *bake*? Wow, you really are getting back to normal."

Katy wasn't sure what constituted "normal" anymore. She might have been possessed by the spirit of Rebecca, Gordon's first wife, but she didn't want to dwell on it. If you started down that road, you began doubting every thought and action until you were deliberately doing things just to be sure you weren't someone else.

As Jett headed down the loft stairs, Katy gave the loft one last scan with the light. She caught movement at the edge of the beam, and she focused it on the scarecrow man. It appeared to be swaying just a little, even though the air in the loft was still.

And she couldn't be sure, but its black-stitched smile seemed to be turned up a bit more in the corners.

Don't start down that road.

She closed the door and followed Jett through the goats, which were now kneeling near one another to sleep.

Like one big happy family.

CHAPTER SIX

Odus Hampton pulled his battered Chevy Blazer into the general store's rutted parking lot. It was a quarter before nine in the morning, which almost guaranteed he'd be Sarah's first customer of the day. He figured on buying a cup of coffee and a honey bun, something to kick the hangover out of his head before he went up to Bethel Springs. In addition to odd jobs, he worked part-time for Crystal Mountain Bottlers, a Greensboro company that siphoned off fresh mountain spring water, shipped it to a factory for treatment, then charged idiots more than a buck a bottle. Even with all those tricks the Arabs were pulling, gas was still cheaper per gallon than the stuff Odus pumped through a hose into Crystal Mountain's tankers.

He stepped from the Blazer with a silent groan, his ligaments tight. Maybe if he stuck to spring water instead of Old Crow bourbon, he wouldn't feel like a sixty-year-old twenty years too soon. He stabbed a Marlboro into his mouth and fired it up, counting the number of steps to the front door to see if he could get half the smoke finished. Even good old Sarah had given in to the "No smoking" bullshit, and though she sold two dozen brands of cigarettes, pipe tobacco, and snuff, she wouldn't let her customers use the products in her store.

That whole tobacco thing was as bad as the Arabs and their gas, only this time it was the federal government turning the screws. Did away with price support so cigarette companies had farmers by the balls, then taxed the devil out of the stuff on the back end.

Odus coughed and spat as he climbed the porch steps. The general store wasn't as grand as it had been in his childhood, when he'd bounced up those steps with a quarter in his pocket and all manner of choices.

A quarter could buy you a Batman comic book and a candy bar, or a Pepsi-Cola and a moon pie, or a pack of baseball cards and a bubble gum cigar. Now all a quarter did was weigh down your pants. And Odus's pants needed all the help they could get, what with his belly pushing down on his belt like a watermelon balanced on a clothesline.

The front door was open. That was funny. Sarah always kept it closed until nine on the dot, but if you were a regular, you could knock and go on in if you showed up a little early. Odus took a final tug of his cigarette and threw it into the sand-filled bucket with all the other unfinished butts. He peered through the screen door, looking for signs of movement.

"Sarah?"

Maybe she was in back, checking on inventory or stacking up some canned preserves that bore the Solom General Store label but were actually contracted to a police auxiliary group over in Westmoreland County. Odus called again. Maybe Sarah had gone over to her house, which sat just beside the store. Decided she'd need a helping of prunes to move things along, maybe. At her age, nature needed a little push now and then.

Odus went to the deli counter at the rear of the store. The coffee pot sat on top in a little blue tray so customers could help themselves. Non-dairy creamer (which was about like non-cow hamburger if you stopped to think about it), straws, white packets of sugar, and pink packets of artificial sweetener were scattered across the tray. The coffee maker was turned off, and the pot was empty and as cold as a witch's heart in December. Sarah always made coffee first thing.

A twinge rippled through Odus's colon, as if a tiny salamander were turning flips down there. It might have been a cheap whiskey fart gathering steam, or it might have been the first stirring of unease. Either way, Odus felt it was time for some fresh morning air.

As he passed the register on the way out, he saw Sarah's frail body curled across a couple of sacks of feed corn. Her eyes were partially open, her mouth slack, a thick strand of drool hanging from one corner of her gray lips.

Odus went around the counter and knelt on the buckled hardwood floor, feeling for her pulse. All he felt was his own, the hangover beating through his thumb. He turned her face up and put his cheek near her mouth. A stagnant breeze stirred, with that peculiar old-person's smell of pine, denture paste, and decay. She was alive.

"Sarah," Odus said, patting her cheek, trying to remember what those emergency techs did in the television shows. All he ever watched were the crime scene shows, and those dealt with people who were already dead. He turned back to the counter and was searching among the candy wrappers, invoices, and business cards for the phone when he heard a soft moan.

Sarah blinked once, a film over her eyes like spider webs. She tried to sit up, but Odus eased her back down.

"Sarah, what happened?"

Her mouth opened, and with her wrinkled neck and glazed eyes, she looked like a fledging robin trying to suck a digested worm from its mother's beak.

"Easy, now," Odus said, his mouth drying, wishing Solom wasn't in the dry part of the county and a cold beer was in the cooler alongside the seventeen kinds of cola.

"*Hat*," Sarah said.

"Yes, ma'am, it's sure hot for September," Odus said. "You must have worked up an early sweat. Overdid it a little. But you just sit and rest now."

Sarah slapped at his chest with a bony hand. "*Haaaat.*"

"I know. I'll get you some water."

Sarah grabbed his forearm, her fingers like the talon of a red hawk. She sat up, her face rigid. "You damned drunken fool," she said, spittle flying from her mouth. "The man in the hat. He's back."

Sarah's eyes closed and she collapsed onto the gray, coarse sacks, her breathing shallow but steady.

Odus renewed his search for the phone. Going on about a hat, of all things. She must have suffered a stroke and blown her senses. Most males in these parts wore a hat, and it wasn't unknown for them to come back now and again.

CHAPTER SEVEN

Maters.

Those blessed tomatoes were going to be the death of her.

Betsy Ward canned, stewed, frozen, and dried about thirty pounds of those red, ugly things. The blight hit hard because of the wet summer, and the first frosts killed the plants, but her husband Arvel brought in a double armload just before the big autumn die-off. Now tomatoes sat in rows across the windowsill, along the counter, and on the pantry shelves, turning from green to pink to full sinful red, with the occasional leaking black spot. The thing about tomatoes was that no bug or cutworm would attack them. The plants were as poisonous as belladonna, and bugs were smart enough to know that maters would kill you. But people were a lot dumber than bugs.

Betsy wiped the sweat away with a dirty towel. She'd been born in Solom and managed to get off the mountain for a year to attend community college. She'd wanted to be a typist then, maybe get on with Westridge University and draw vacation and retirement. But Arvel had come along with his pick-up and Doc Watson tapes and rusty mufflers and he'd seemed like the Truth for a nineteen-year-old mountain girl, and then one night he forgot the rubber and nine months later they were married and the baby came out with the cord wrapped around its neck. They tried a few times after that, but now all they had was a long piece of property and a garden and so many tomatoes that Betsy wanted to grab Arvel's shotgun and blow them all to puree.

She looked out the window and saw Gordon's widow checking the mailbox. Even after more than a year on the farm, the woman still wore that big-city, washed-out look, as if she couldn't wander into daylight without a full plate of make-up. Still, she seemed harmless enough, and not as standoffish as the other outsiders who had flooded the valley since Betsy's knee-high days. And Betsy was sick to death of her kitchen, anyway. She flicked the slimy seeds from her fingers and headed for the door, determined to gossip with her neighbor.

Three mailboxes stood at the mouth of the gravel drive. Arvel's place was the closest to the highway, followed by the Smith farm, then by a plot owned by a fellow Betsy never met, although she'd peeked in his mailbox and learned that his name was Alex Eakins. A pretty young woman drove by to visit him about once a week or so, probably up to fornication and other sins.

"Howdy," Betsy called from the porch.

The redhead looked up from the box where she was thumbing through a stack of envelopes. Her eyes were bloodshot and weepy-looking. Betsy wondered if she was a drinker. Gordon Smith wouldn't have stood for too much of that behavior, even though he turned out not to be as harmless as everyone in Solom—Betsy included—had figured.

"Hi, Mrs. Ward," She smiled with nice, straight city teeth. Her ankles were way too skinny and would probably snap plumb in half if she ever hitched a mule to a plow and cut a straight furrow. Still, she looked a little tough, like a piece of rawhide that had been licked and stuck out in the sun. And she'd walked the quarter-mile to the mailbox instead of jumping in a car. "How are the tomatoes this year?"

"The Lord was way too good to us," Betsy, thinking the exact opposite, but such things weren't said in God-fearing country. "How you liking Solom these days?"

"We're getting used to it. A little different from Charlotte, though."

Betsy wasn't so sure the redhead meant that first part, since the corners of her mouth were turned down and her eyes twitched like she hadn't got a wink of sleep. "So you and your girl gonna be staying on a while longer?"

"We don't know yet. The case may go to court."

"Then it's going to depend on which judge you get. Johnson is an honest man, but Overcash is related to the Smiths. You'd probably lose out if he's holding the gavel."

"We're just taking it day by day," the woman said. Betsy knew the woman had stayed with the name of Katy Logan, because she'd never taken the Smith name in matrimony, and her daughter carried a different name yet. Big-city nonsense, that's what it was. Who could keep up with who?

Betsy also knew the woman subscribed to foolish magazines like *Money, National Geographic,* and *Time* when she should have been reading the farmer's almanac and seed catalogs. A woman who stuffed her head with information instead of wisdom was doomed in Solom. And Katy had survived one close call already.

She might not be so lucky when the Horseback Preacher came back around. Especially since Harmon Smith was Gordon's ancestor and just might want to lay his own claim to the family land.

Arvel's border collie, Digger, dragged itself from under the shade of the porch and stood by the steps, giving a bark to show he'd been on duty all along.

"Solom's beautiful this time of year," the redhead said. She turned her face to the sun and breathed deeply. "All these mountains and fresh air. It's still a little strange at night to fall asleep without lights burning everywhere."

"Oh, we got lights," Betsy said. "God's lights. Them little specks in the sky."

The redhead stopped by Betsy's gate. Digger sniffed and growled.

"Hold back, Digger," Betsy said. "It's neighbors."

"The constellations," the redhead said, her face flushing a little. "You can see them all the way down to the horizon. In my old neighborhood, you saw maybe four stars at night."

"I don't mean to pry, but how's Jett's dad?" Betsy most certainly did mean to pry, but she figured the Lord would forgive a little white lie in service of a greater good.

"He's fully recovered now, although his left arm is not as strong as it used to be. He says it's all history now."

History just means you lived too long, Betsy thought. *Valley families have made their peace with the past. And with the Horseback Preacher. The families that are still around, anyhow.*

In a way, Betsy admired Katy standing up to her husband, even if it defied the Old Testament. Why, if Betsy so much as opened her mouth in anger to Arvel, he would slap her across the cheek and send her to the floor. In the Free Will church, she kept her trap shut except for the occasional hymn or moan of praise, and she sat to the left with the other wives and the children. It was important to know your place in God's scheme of things. First there was God, then the Horseback Preacher, and then the husband.

Still, the skinny woman caused two men to fight to the death over her. The fact that one was a lunatic and the other a drughead didn't make it any less impressive.

Katy not only walked away a widow, she'd done it to the tune of a property deed. Maybe Betsy could learn a thing or two from *her.*

Digger growled again, sensing Betsy's unease.

"How's Jett liking school?" she asked, happy to change the

subject.

"Okay so far. You know how kids are."

Betsy knew, despite never having raised one. "It's tough at that age when the boys start sniffing around. Like Digger here after a bone, but nowhere near as genuine."

Katy laughed. "I think she can take care of herself."

If you two stood up to Gordon Smith gone crazy with a scythe and the Horseback Preacher all in the same night, I don't much doubt that at all.

"Well, I'd best get back to my canning."

"Could you show me how to do it someday?"

"Sure thing." Though Betsy had no intention of giving away any family secrets.

"It's supposed to be a cold winter, so it's good to stock up."

Betsy gave her an appraising look. Maybe she wasn't so dumb after all. "Squirrels hoarding like crazy, the stripes on the woolly worms are mostly black, and August was foggy as all get-out. Signs like that means bad weather ahead.

"Well, best to be prepared either way." Katy waved and added a "Good doggie" for Digger's sake, although Digger was having none of it. Betsy left the dog on the porch to encourage Katy on her way. The bony woman made her way up the gravel road, grabbing at the goldenrod that bloomed along the ditch.

"Trouble," Betsy muttered to herself. "A skinny woman ain't never been nothing but trouble."

CHAPTER EIGHT

October was a melancholy month for Alex Eakins.

It was the month his childhood mutt rolled himself under the wheels of a Fed Ex van, the month he'd lost his virginity after a high school football game to a girl who later ditched him for a married man, the month his dad and mom separated, the month he'd been kicked out of Duke for lousy grades and poor attendance. Since he'd moved to the mountains and spent his trust fund on a little piece of south-facing land on the mountain above Solom, this had always been a season of dying.

He sniffed the air, which was sweet with the sugar of red maples and crabapples. The stench of decay should have been there, but the only rot came from the black innards of his composting toilet, where bacteria performed its thankless job of turning shit to dirt. Nature was just beginning to accept that winter was on the way, that every living thing would soon be asleep or dead. He wondered which of those he would be.

Alex embraced organic gardening as a lifestyle, earning enough by selling produce at the county farmer's market to pay his property taxes. He studied all the latest sustainable building techniques, and his own house was a mix of technologies both primitive and new. Since he lived off-grid and wasn't beholden to the building inspection and permitting process, Alex used cob and straw bale construction for much of his house, which was cut partly into the bank for better heat retention.

From the outside, the structure looked as much like an

aboriginal mud hut as anything, but it was highly energy efficient. A small cluster of solar panels on the roof ran a compact refrigerator, and a wood stove system circulated hot water through the house. Alex had fixed a generator to a paddle wheel in the creek that gushed along one side of his property. The generator, along with a miniature wind turbine, fed a bank of alternating-current batteries, so he was covered no matter what the weather.

The system was put together in the aftermath of Y2K, when all the doomsayers realized the world wasn't going to end after all and sold their survival gear on the cheap. Well, the world may have ended already, for all Alex knew. Because it was autumn again, and the tomatoes were turning to mush on the vines and the corn was getting hard. The cool-weather greens like collards, spinach, and turnips still had a few weeks to go, but soon enough the market would close for the season. Alex had a truckload of pumpkins to sell for Halloween, and one more good haul of organic broccoli, but after that, he would have to go back to work. Or else sell a little of the marijuana he cultivated.

But that meant dealing with people.

The same idiotic people who had driven him to the isolation of his mountain retreat. Despite the added pleasure of end-running the government and the lure of the world's last free-market economy, selling dope was almost as much trouble as having a square job. When all of that ruckus erupted on the Smith farm last year and cops were everywhere, Alex was sure he'd end up getting busted, but they'd merely questioned him about Gordon Smith's death.

After he'd played the "See no evil, hear no evil, speak no evil" stoned monkey for them, they'd left him alone. But he learned enough to figure out the professor was killed by his wife's first husband. Sounded like some kind of soap-opera shit, but you had to admire a guy who burned with that kind of passion, even though they'd eventually ruled the death a case of self-defense. But all those rumors about Gordon dressing up as a scarecrow were kind of creepy.

Alex dumped a bucket of table scraps onto his garden compost heap and looked over the valley below. The trees were just starting to turn color along the highway, where the roots were stressed by construction and carbon monoxide. A gravel road ran past the Ward and Smith houses before disappearing into the thicket and winding up to Alex's house.

The road got a lot bumpier and rutted past the Smith farm, because Alex believed in inhibiting curiosity-seekers. Not because he was antisocial as his mom claimed, or a stubborn asshole as his dad claimed, but because he didn't have the patience to deal with accidental tourists and uninvited guests. Plus, the government might have an interest in finding him.

Besides, he wasn't antisocial. Just ask Meredith, the earth chick he'd met at the farmer's market who'd occupied half of his bed on and off since April. But April was a green month and October was red and golden, so he expected her to light out before the first big frost.

Her voice came from the wooden deck. "Honey?"

Honey. That reminded him, next year he planned on setting up a honeybee hive. With all the pests that attacked honeybees, the real stuff was getting more and more valuable. Alex was sure he could do it right, and have the fringe benefit of his own tiny, winged army of blossom pollinators—

"Alex?"

He put down the scrap bucket and picked up the heavy hoe. "Yes, dear?"

"Are you mad at me about something?"

"Of course not." Down below, through the trees, a thread of gray smoke rose from the Ward chimney.

"You only call me 'Dear' when you're mad at me."

"That's not so."

"And you say it out the side of your mouth, like you're talking on automatic or something. Like you're miles away."

Gasoline was pushing four bucks a gallon, thanks to the military-industrial complex that ruled the country, and that had to be factored against the profit from a load of pumpkins. Maybe he'd drive the load to Westridge. The college kids had plenty of money. He should know, as much grass as he'd peddled to them over the last couple of years. "Everything's fine, dear."

"See? There you go again."

"Huh?"

"You said 'Dear' again."

He turned and squinted up at the deck. The day was bright, though cool. Meredith stood in a gray terry-cloth robe, her blonde hair wet and steaming. No doubt she was nude beneath, and Alex thought of those nipples that were the color and consistency of pencil erasers. He could almost smell her shampoo, the hippie-dippy expensive stuff she bought at the health food store. He tightened his grip on the hoe.

"Sorry," he said. "I was thinking about autumn."

"Like, fall?"

"Yeah. Everything's dying but there's a promise of rebirth. It's metaphorical."

"Alex, have you been in the stash?"

"Did you know that most leaves aren't really green? The chlorophyll in the leaves masks their true color, and when the growing process slows down for autumn, the chlorophyll fades and the true color emerges. It's the process of dying that finally reveals the leaf. So all that green, happy horseshit is a lie."

"Alex? Are you okay?"

Sure, he was okay. He'd been okay for years. Marijuana was his antidepressant, and his crop kept him supplied year-round. He also traded on the black market to support his other little hobby-the one locked in the walk-in closet downstairs — but figured he'd probably get caught one day and the cops would seize his land.

All because he liked to smoke a little weed, which was none of the government's business besides the fact that it kept neo-cons in office with their permanent War on Drugs. At least weed was honest, though the system wasn't. Weed stayed green, even after it was dead, even after you smoked it and it grew a bouquet of blossoms in your head.

True colors don't stay hidden for long.

Meredith smoked it, too, but only before bed, because it made her terribly horny. In fact, Alex often wondered if that was the sole reason she stayed over that night in April, and then the next night, and before the end of the week she'd begun leaving her clothes in his dresser. And that, as any guy knew, was the time to say he wasn't sure they were ready for such a commitment, but another joint and Alex's head was diving between her thighs and, well, he supposed it could be worse. At least she could cook vegan.

He smiled up at her, or maybe he was grimacing from dawn's glare in his eyes. "I'm fine," he said. "I was just wondering whether to take the pumpkins down to the college or try my luck at the market."

"The market's been a little slow, and some of the other vendors will probably undercut you. Better to go where there's no competition."

"Makes sense." Meredith possessed a business degree, graduating *cum laude* the year before with a degree in marketing. Alex had majored in botany, but all he'd learned was how to grow some high-class, kick-ass grass. And how to flunk out and disappoint his parents.

"Are you going into town?" Meredith asked. "Town" meant Titusville, the Pickett County seat, which was fifteen miles away. No one thought of Solom as a town, although it had a zip code and post office. Titusville was where people did their serious shopping, and the Solom General Store was a place to pop in for vegetable seeds, or a bag of Fritos corn chips and a Snickers bar when the munchies got extreme.

"Maybe later," he said. He never wore a watch, and if he was forced to get a part-time gig for the winter, that meant showing up according to some corporate master's rigid timetable. Time was flexible and shouldn't be tied down to numbers.

Like, this was now and later was later, and yesterday was like the ashes and grunge in the bottom of the bong. And, tomorrow was, like, maybe a pot seed or something.

"Well, then, what do you want to do this fine Saturday morning?" Meredith leaned over the deck, letting her robe fall open and offering a generous view that rivaled the glory of the Blue Ridge Mountains.

He grinned, or maybe a gnat was flitting near his eyes. "Roll one and I'll come up in a minute."

She smiled. "Breakfast in bed?"

"Sure—" He started to add "dear," but caught himself.

Meredith padded across the deck Alex built with his own two hands using wormy chestnut planks he'd taken from an abandoned barn. Maybe Meredith belonged here. She was organic in her way, wasn't spoiled by modern conveniences, and had grown on him over the months. He just couldn't understand why, as she'd talked to him, his grip on the hoe tightened. He looked down and saw that his knuckles were white.

"Yes, dear," he whispered, chopping at a plantain that had

taken root by the garden. Plantains carried the same blight that killed tomatoes in wet weather. They were evil weeds if God had ever made such a thing.

Alex lifted the hoe for a second blow when he saw a skewed stand of stalks at the end of his garden. Something had been in his corn. He stepped over the rows of broccoli and walked past the beds of young spinach, his blood rising to a boil. The corn was trampled and the tops bitten off a number of the plants. Deer sometimes came through the woods to feast on the garden, though their visits dwindled after Alex picked up a tip from a fellow organic gardener. A little human piss around the garden's perimeter kept deer away, because as dumb as the dark-eyed creatures were, they'd been around long enough to associate people with murder.

This wasn't deer damage. Because a slew of stalks were littered along the fence that separated his property line from the Smith farm.

Alex was ambivalent about fences, since Starship Earth belonged to everybody, although he'd made damned sure he knew his property boundaries after the survey was complete. He believed in the laws of Nature, but that didn't mean the rest of his nasty, grab-assed species did. They believed in pieces of paper in the courthouse, or pieces of paper in banks, or pieces of paper in Washington, D.C.

But, paper or not, one thing was for sure: goats couldn't read, and even if they could, Alex would bet half a kilo of homegrown that they would ignore what was written on the deed anyway. He kept a tight grip on the hoe just in case one of the weird-eyed bastards was still around.

The wire fence was bent just a little, as if something heavy had leaned on it. Heavier than a goat, by the looks of it. Alex hesitated. He tried to live in harmony with the world, even if six-and-a-half billion hairless apes threatened to make the place uninhabitable. He could either go down and have a talk with Gordon Smith's widow, or he could cross no-man's land into enemy territory and administer some mountain justice.

"Alexxxxxx!" From the purr in Meredith's voice, Alex guessed she'd already fired up the joint. He dropped the hoe.

"I'll be back," he said to the woods beyond the fence.

CHAPTER NINE

"Don't get any ideas," Katy said as she pulled the Subaru up to Mark's rental cabin.

Jett looked over from the passenger seat with a twinkle her in eye. "What kind of ideas?"

"You know."

"Hey, you're the one that fell in love with him and bred."

"That was a long time ago and things happened."

Addiction happened. Emotional distance happened. Divorce happened. And then the long and winding road led to Gordon Smith and this haunted piece of Solom real estate she couldn't afford to abandon, even with all the controversy and whispers and suspicion.

"Well, now it's now and new things can happen," Jett said.

"That ship not only sailed, it took on water and broke up on the shoals, honey."

"I see the way you look at him."

Mark came out on the cabin porch and waved. She couldn't help the way she looked at him. "It's because I see you in him. Nothing will ever change that."

Jett leaned over and kissed Katy on the cheek, which surprised her. Jett was in a bit of a "no touchy" phase, especially in front of other people. As Jett opened the door and slid out of the car, Katy wondered if maybe the affection was a little show for Mark.

She rolled her window down. "I'll be back in two hours."

"Why don't you join us?" Mark said.

He looked healthy and tan, his hair ruffled as if he'd been out splitting firewood. The outdoor jobs he'd taken combined with his recovery to fill out the shoulders of his plaid shirt. His jeans seemed to fit better, too, not that she could afford a full survey. She could almost smell him, at least the memory of him.

"Some other time," she said. "I've got errands."

She drove away before he could respond, glancing in the rearview mirror to see if he was watching. But he'd already draped his arm around Jett to lead her into the cabin, where they'd have lunch and play Boggle and listen to Jett's new favorite band, Death Cab for Cutie. According to Jett, Mark had taken an interest in bluegrass and traditional mountain music and even bought himself a dulcimer.

Katy wasn't sure if his transformation was all an act. Perhaps risking his life for them awakened him to the things he truly valued. Or maybe this was just another mask, one as creepy as Gordon Smith's hideous burlap sack with the burned-out eyeholes.

The drive to Windshake was pleasant, affording her a chance to appreciate the Blackburn River Valley and the autumnal splendor of the wooded slopes. The hayfields were golden with a ripe harvest, but the gardens were down to little more than cabbages and pole beans. Cattle milled across the lowland pastures, the herds not yet thinned for the winter. Despite temperatures in the sixties, thin gray threads of smoke arose from the occasional farmhouse chimney.

Titusville was the county seat, but only because it was the geographic center of the county. Its population was barely ten thousand, although a business strip had grown up along the route to the county courthouse, sheriff's department, jail, and hospital. The usual chain outlets had popped up their standardized presences, with Wal-Mart, Lowe's Home

Improvement, Dollar General, and McDonald's joining the few locally owned small businesses that struggled to survive in their shadows.

She parked at the courthouse, easily finding a parking spot. No meters, either. In Charlotte, parking was a blood sport and often required the giving of a kidney.

The desk clerk in the sheriff's office recognized her—of course she would, considering Katy was the most sensational thing to happen to county law enforcement in years—and said, "He's waiting, Mrs. Smith, please go on in."

"It's 'Logan,'" she said, keeping it pleasant despite her annoyance. Hadn't her name been on enough police reports, court documents, and newspaper pages?

Sheriff Frank Littlefield was waiting by his office door and ushered her in. He was tall and strong-jawed but not a caricature of the country cop, with a thin face, working-class hands, and a hound dog aspect to his eyes that made him seem constantly sad. She'd heard he'd endured some tragedies of his own. Or maybe he was dismayed to see her again.

"We have no new information, Ms. Logan," he said, waiting for her to sit before settling behind his desk. "No motive for your husband's behavior."

"I know his family has deep roots here, and I understand you want to downplay the whole thing," she said, choosing her words carefully, She didn't want to accuse him of a cover-up, because she was just as happy if no one dug too deeply, or she'd have to start testifying about headless ghosts and a supernatural preacher seeking vengeance. "We're eager to move on, too."

He scratched the buzz cut above one ear. "All the evidence backed up your story," he said. "If not for your first husband's criminal record, it probably would have wrapped up faster, but you know how people are. Especially as respected as the Smith family name is. I couldn't let people think I buried it."

"That's odd. From what I can tell, most people in Solom weren't all that surprised when Gordon Smith was skewered by a wooden pole out in his own cornfield."

"People talk," Sheriff Littlefield said. "Those old stories about Harmon Smith have been around forever."

"And I gather every time somebody dies mysteriously or violently, old Harmon gets the credit."

"There haven't been many on my watch," the sheriff said, with a touch of defiance, as if he couldn't be expected to protect his constituents from the creatures of legend.

"One of them was on your watch, though. Gordon's first wife Rebecca."

The sheriff stretched out his palms facedown on his desk. "Now, that was an open-and-shut case. Single-occupant car accident. She drove off in the gulley there at the farm one night and cut her head clean off."

"That night last year, Gordon bragged about killing her. And when a man's waving a bloody scythe at you, it's easy to believe such a statement."

"I don't think any of us will ever know what really went down on the Smith farm," the sheriff said, in a tone of veiled accusation as if he knew Katy hadn't told the whole story. Or maybe he was just letting her know that he and Solom were just as glad if the real truth were never known.

"I've heard the gossip," Katy said.

"Look, if some townies and farmer's wives want to blame everything on the return of the Horseback Preacher, coming 'round to reap some souls or whatever, then that's okay with me. I did my job and in the end, justice was served. Maybe not under the law of the land, but some laws are bigger than a courthouse and a country sheriff."

"I just want to honor Rebecca's memory," Katy said. "We were both deceived by the same man. I'm sure you can appreciate the kinship there."

"Family mess, ma'am. One thing that never changes in Solom, Testers will be Testers, Smiths will be Smiths, and the Blackburn River just keeps sliding on by to the ocean."

"So whatever happens behind closed doors is fine as long as you don't get accused of a cover-up?"

His cheeks reddened with anger. "I've gone the extra mile for you and Mark Draper. Some folks would have been happy to lynch him, and others wanted to give him a medal and elect him mayor. The fact that he stuck around proves he has some pluck, but maybe you should kindly encourage him that it's time to move on. I can work it out with his probation officer."

"Just like that," she said. "It's over?"

"It's over. If it ever even happened."

Katy stood to leave without waiting for him to play the gentleman and escort her out. "I'll tell Rebecca, next time I see her."

CHAPTER TEN

Sarah Jeffers came to her senses in a dimly lighted room. At first, she thought she was in her bed on the second floor of the old family home by the store, because the light through the window projected a late-Sunday-morning quality. Sunday was her sleep-in day, and her headache might have been caused by a couple of tall after-dinner sherries. Her eyelids were heavy, so she listened for the ticking of the antique grandfather clock downstairs. She heard nothing but a faint, irregular beeping.

And the smell was all wrong. Instead of aged wood, musty quilts, and cats, the room carried the crisp tang of antiseptic. She opened her eyes and blinked her vision into focus. The walls were white, unlike the maple paneling of her bedroom. The pillows were encased in vinyl and the bed was angled up like a lounge chair at the side of a swimming pool.

"Back among the living," a young woman said. "How do you feel?"

"Get me a doctor," Sarah said.

The woman smiled. "I *am* a doctor. Dr. Hyatt. You're in Tri-Cities Regional Hospital."

Sarah closed her eyes. Doctors were supposed to be male and gray-haired. How could this urchin know the least little thing about the workings of the human body? She didn't look old enough to have ever pulled the legs off a grasshopper, much less gone through medical school.

"One of your friends found you at your store," Dr. Hyatt said. "You were unconscious."

"And that's a bad thing, right?"

"A sense of humor. Good. 'Laughter is the best medicine' is not just a section in *Reader's Digest*. The claim also has some research backing it up."

"Then tell me a good one so I can laugh my way out of this thousand-dollar-an-hour prison cell. Let me out of here."

"It's not that simple, Miss Jeffers. It *is* 'Miss,' isn't it?"

"I can't lay around here during store hours. I got customers to see to."

"We ran some tests while you were unconscious. You presented symptoms of a stroke, but your EEG and CAT were fine and your blood pressure is that of somebody thirty years younger."

"Tests? Who signed for them? And why are these wires sticking into me?"

"The gentleman who called 9-1-1 said you have no next of kin. We followed the usual procedures for treating an apparent stroke victim."

"But I ain't been stroked, have I?"

"Not that we can tell. We thought you might have suffered a blow to the head, maybe by a food can falling from a top shelf. Or a robbery. But the register was untouched and the store appeared to be intact. Your friend called the Sheriff's Department and they checked it out. And you have no visible marks. My initial diagnosis is a sudden onset of reverse endorphins, a mild form of shock."

Sarah struggled to sit up, saw black spots before her eyes, and decided to try again a little later. "I hope somebody locked up. Half the merchandise will walk off otherwise."

"The deputies will take care of that. Your job is to get better."

The black spots coalesced behind her eyelids, turning into a shadow—a man in a black, wide-brimmed hat. She reached out for the doctor's arm and clutched it, afraid the image would still be there if she opened her eyes. The beeping accelerated.

"Are you okay, Miss Jeffers?"

"I seen him," she said.

"Your friend? He said you were unconscious, but you might have been partially aware of what was going on. It's not unusual during a fainting spell."

"No, *before* that. I seen him." Suddenly she wasn't in such a big hurry to leave Titusville and go back to Solom.

"Just breathe regularly," Dr. Hyatt said, patting Sarah's hand until the beep marking her pulse became steady again. "Rest up. You're not going anywhere for a little while."

That sounded good to Sarah. She closed her eyes and tried to block the recurring image of the man tilting up his chin until the wide brim no longer hid his face.

Or what was *left* of his face.

CHAPTER ELEVEN

Alex Eakins parked his pick-up at the edge of the woods, below an embankment along his property line. He finished the last of his joint and doused the roach. He almost tossed it in the ashtray for later, but if a cop found it there, that would probably constitute grounds for a search warrant. The fucking pigs were just that way, and they'd gotten a lot porkier under the *nouveau* fascism of the Bushbama regime.

Fuck them all. Fuck the jug-eared, big-budget president and his totalitarian, snooping ways. Fuck the spineless liberals who curled up in a ball as they were kicked, and fuck even his chosen Libertarian Party for lacking the charm to capture the popular imagination. When it really counted, political action wasn't broadcast babble and social-media bullshit, it was up close and personal—hands on.

He retrieved his Pearson Freedom compound bow and arrows from the back seat and wandered to the fence. The Smith goats grazed and browsed among the scrub vegetation, eating blackberry vines, pine trees, locusts, and pokeweed, not caring what entered their mouths as long as it was green or brown. Alex considered having a neighborly talk with Smith's widow, but that might lead to unexpected visits and nosing around, and then maybe a peek into the little shed behind Alex's mud house.

Besides, it was the *goats* that fucked with his garden, not their owner. So it was the goats that had to pay. Alex notched an arrow and tilted the bow, then pinched and stretched the string back, muscles straining against the taut arc of the bow.

It was power, primitive and raw and heady. Or maybe he was stoned.

The herd of nearly a dozen gave him a speculative appraisal when he'd parked, but the animals now returned to their chewing. The nearest goat was thirty yards away, peeling the bark from a bare sapling. It was tan and white, ears long and funneled, horns curved and short. The age of goats was hard to figure, since they got plump and grew beards before they were a year old, but Alex figured this one for middle age. Probably was bound for the meat locker this winter.

Well, the day of reckoning was coming a little ahead of schedule.

Goaticide, dude. In mass quantities.

Alex sighted down the arrow, aiming just a little high to compensate for the natural pull of gravity. He was about to let fly when he sensed movement in a prickly grove of crabapples behind the herd. Somebody was walking toward him. *Shit.* Must be that redneck goon Odus Hampton, the odd-jobber who hung around down at the general store. Odus did chores around the Smith place in exchange for liquor money and crops, and probably harbored some sort of inbred devotion to his bosses.

Mountain folk like Odus clung to the ideals their Irish and Scots ancestors brought to the mountains as they fled for the freedom of the Southern Appalachians. They were driven by a rebellious streak, but still measured themselves against the value systems of their oppressive overlords and would do anything for a dollar.

Or maybe Odus was just drunk and rambling. For his ilk, all the roads led nowhere.

Alex eased the tension on the string and leaned against the camouflage to wait for Odus to move on. The goats didn't turn toward Odus's approach, which didn't make sense. If Odus was the one who regularly fed them, they should have gone running at the first sniff of his bourbon-sweet stench.

Alex peeked from his concealment. It wasn't Odus coming down the dirt path.

It was a man in a hat and an ill-cut suit that was too short for his arms. He wore a ragged black tie that was cut in the shape of a cross, and his white linen shirt looked like a stained tooth against the grimy topcoat. His bony wrists were exposed, along with a couple of inches of pale forearm. He wore square-toed leather boots and his woolen pants were riddled with tiny rips and moth holes. His face was hidden in the shade of the hat's oversize brim.

Whoa. "Twilight Zone" material, weird dude walking.

Alex debated getting back into his truck and driving away, but the man would probably see him carrying the bow. The stranger wouldn't know Alex had been about to kill a goat, but he might tell the Smith widow about the encounter. She might report Alex to the sheriff's department as a trespasser, and they would come with a warrant whether Alex was guilty or not.

That's just the way the fucking cops were, they made up a silly reason to investigate you so they could find something serious to bust you over. It was the same whether your broken tail light led to a drunk-driving arrest or a bogus trespassing claim got you nailed for illegal manufacture of a Schedule I narcotic.

Alex decided to wait it out. Maybe the stranger was trespassing, too, and would walk amid the herd and head to the road. Weird Dude Walking could just walk the hell right on off the stage.

But the stranger didn't keep walking. He stopped in the middle of the herd, in a cleared area of trampled goldenrod and tickseed. The man tilted his head forward so that even the shadow of his face was hidden by the battered hat's brim. He folded his hands in front of him and stood as still as a scarecrow. The goats stopped their ruminating and turned to him, one by one. The only sounds were the October breeze skirling dead leaves and the ticking of the truck's engine as it cooled. Even the crows fell hushed in the high treetops.

The goat closest to Alex, the one he planned to murder, took a few steps toward the man in the hat. It emitted a soft bleat. Another of the goats, farther up the hill, echoed the bleat, and then others joined in. It wasn't the yearning bleat that hungry goats often made. These calls were gentle and almost tender, like the sound a kid would make as it nestled its mother's teats.

Weird Dude Walking slowly lifted his arms until they were suspended straight out from the sides of his body. It looked as if he were imitating a giant bird and would at any moment start flapping for takeoff. But his movements were slow and graceful, like those of someone at peace.

The goats all moved forward at the same time, headed for the stranger. The largest, a fat old billy with a long, filthy beard, reached him first and sniffed at the wool suit. The man remained perfectly still, though his body seemed to relax a little, his limp hands dangling from the ends of his raised arms. Other goats crowded around, their nostrils flaring as they checked the air.

The nearest goat bumped its nose against the man's coat, then opened its jaws and took the cloth in its mouth. The man kept his head tilted and made no sign of movement. The goats squeezed closer, and now others poked their snouts against his skin. The big billy tugged on the coat, first gently and then harder, until a lower button popped free. The other goats nipped at the fabric, yanking their heads back with the clothing clenched between their jaws, their bleats growing more frantic.

Alex wondered if Weird Dude wore worn some sort of scent that attracted the goats. Deer hunters would splash their coveralls with buck urine, hoping to entice does from the woods. Maybe the biotech corporations had invented a special scent to attract goats. Alex fell back on the theory that the man had fed the goats before and they associated his scent with grain or sugar.

Desperate goat mouths ripped open Weird Dude Walking's coat, the bone buttons sparkling in the sun as they arced to the ground. The man wore a flannel long john shirt underneath, but it was shredded in places and deathly pale skin showed through the openings. The goats tugged on the man but he kept his balance. Alex wondered why Weird Dude didn't push the animals away.

Like he wants it to happen.

The man's arms were pulled down, and one of the sleeves was yanked free. Two goats played tug-of-war with the wool coat, and then jerked it off the man's back. The coat settled on a patch of dried-up goldenrod. Weird Dude finally lifted his face and Alex expected either the awe-inspiring expression of a Mushroom God or else a Charlie Sheen smirk. From fifty yards away, all Alex could tell was that Weird Dude looked sick, his skin unhealthy and sallow. But a smile creased his pasty face as he looked at the sky and endured the hircine assault.

The goats became frantic, their teeth tearing the man's clothes, and Alex almost left his hidden vantage point and went to the rescue. If Weird Dude acted in any way alarmed, Alex would empty his quiver of arrows into the goats. But his unnatural serenity caused Alex to watch and wait.

Dude's making his choice. None of my business.

The goats ripped until Weird Dude's flannel underwear gave way, and then one of the goats bit deep into the man's side. The man should have screamed, but the smile didn't waver as the goat worked its head back and forth, trying to pull the piece of flesh free. Another goat went for the soft portion of the stomach just below the navel and backed away, a string of meat dangling from its mouth.

Alex gripped the tree in front of him, the bark scraping his cheek and his breath so loud he was sure the goats could hear it above their own noise. A mantra came to him, in a dull throb that mirrored his accelerated pulse: *Not happening, not happening, not happening*. And then came the syncopated accent beat: *No way in hell happening*.

Instead of blood spilling from Weird Dude's wounds, a milky substance oozed out, thick as cottage cheese. The goats bit into the man, and one butted him in the left thigh, causing him to lean to one side. A dirty brown goat grabbed the outstretched arm as the man tried to regain his balance. Its teeth clamped on the wrist and dragged the man toward the ground, the black hat flying from the man's head and landing in the trampled vegetation. Once the man was on his knees, the goats clambered over him, rending the flesh of his neck and back. Not once did the man cry out.

The goats' bleats grew muffled as their mouths filled. They fed on the clabbered juice that leaked from the man's torn flesh.

Weird Dude Walking ain't fucking walking anymore.

Alex broke from the trance that seemed to have fallen over him as he watched the bizarre spectacle. This was no psychedelic vision, this was an ass-end-up slab of reality. He gripped his bow and arrows and stepped from his cover. "Hey," he shouted.

The goats kept feeding. Weird Dude was buried beneath

the mass of dirty, furry animals that were now in a feeding frenzy. The bearded billy backed out of the herd with a prize, a swinging slab of meat that looked like the man's cheek. No blood leaked from the ripped skin, only a few dribbles of moon-white liquid.

Another goat tottered away, dragging what looked to be the strip of a forearm, complete with gleaming bone. A third dipped its head into the downed man's belly and came up with a swollen rope of intestines decorating its blunt horns like a Satanic Christmas trimming.

Alex fought an urge to vomit. The vestiges of the morning's bong hits faded. No buzz was deep enough to mask the insane scene that played out before him. Fuckers didn't just crawl out of the weeds and get eaten by goats. Didn't happen. Maybe in a video game, maybe in a shitty direct-to-video horror movie, but certainly not here on the slopes above Solom, where the Bible thumpers said God was closer than ever and the sky weighed three thousand pounds and the government didn't meddle too much and *NO FUCKING WAY IN THE WORLD WAS WEIRD DUDE GETTING REAMED BY GOATS!!!!*

Alex debated his options. He could charge into the midst of the herd and scatter them, but as much meat as they'd stripped from Weird Dude, Alex didn't see any way the man could still be alive. He had four arrows, so he could thin the herd a little, except then they might turn their eye to fresh prey.

And he knew how goats were—once they got a taste for something, they gobbled it until it was extinct. The third option made the most sense: back the hell away, get in the truck, and pretend this was all a hallucination. Forget reporting the incident to the authorities, because authority equaled government equaled search warrants.

When he started the truck, one of the goats looked up from the corpse and stared in the direction of the noise. A couple of maggot-white fingers protruded between the twisting lips. The goat looked right through the windshield and met his eyes.

Alex was probably just stoned—yeah, that *had* to be it—because there was no way the goat could have been grinning. Either he was stoned or else he'd cracked, and he was too rational to crack.

As the truck bounced up the pitted mountain road, Alex realized that Weird Dude Walking, even while the goats were eviscerating him, hadn't uttered a single sound.

CHAPTER TWELVE

The doctor must have dosed her with some sort of horse pill, because Sarah Jeffers awoke with a mild headache. The sun was already streaming low through the window, so it must have been mid-morning. She hadn't dreamed at all, and her tongue was thick and sticky in her mouth. It took her a moment to remember where she was.

She peeled the sheet off her chest. She was dressed in a baby-poop-green gown tied loosely behind her back. Her clothes were folded in a chair at the foot of the steel-railed bed. So somebody had seen her naked, probably for the first time in at least twenty years. Served them right. They had no business poking around in her innards anyway.

She lay there, calculating yesterday's lost profits. She should have called in one of the Hancocks, or the boy who swept up after school. Even paying somebody a full day's wages, she would have netted fifty bucks at the least. And you never knew when a tourist bus was going to pull up, or a pack of Christian Harley riders.

This time of year, with the fall colors starting to come on, the general store needed to bank enough to get her through the winter. As frightened as she was by the return of the Horseback Preacher, she was more afraid of losing the seasonal profit that would carry her through the lean winter.

A new doctor came in, a man with a mustache that looked penciled over his lip who looked more like a game-show host than somebody in the medical field. It was getting so you couldn't peg people anymore.

"Morning, Miss Jeffers. I'm Doctor Vincent." The doctor put a wrist to her forehead and checked the tension on the clip attached to her finger. Apparently that little clip fed a lot of information to the video monitor on the wall. All the signs appeared to be jagging up and down in some kind of steady pattern.

"Am I fit to go?" Sarah was going to ask for a cup of orange juice but figured that would probably run her five bucks. She was on Medicare but she'd still be stuck with her twenty percent of the bill, meaning the juice would cost her a buck out-of-pocket. She wasn't that thirsty.

"Everything looks good," the doctor said. "You had a rough patch for a little bit, but all your signs are stable. We've diagnosed exhaustion."

"I took on a spell," Sarah said. "I'm all better now, like you said."

"I'll sign your discharge papers, but I urge you to get some extra rest in the next few weeks. I wouldn't want you coming back in with something more serious."

"Don't you worry. I haven't spent so much time in bed since my honeymoon, and that was before you were born."

The doctor almost grinned. "One thing ... while you were out, you were muttering 'Harm me,' over and over again. Did you think somebody was going to hurt you?"

Sarah let her face slip into a mask of cool stone. "Nobody's going to hurt me. I can take care of myself."

"Of that, I have no doubt." He patted her hand. "I'll have the nurse help you get your things together. Do you have someone to drive you home?"

"I'll call somebody."

"Good. Extra sleep for a while. Promise?"

"Sure, Doc."

He left the room, and Sarah lay there in the stink of

antiseptic. The beeping of the monitor accelerated and the jaggedy lines on the screen became erratic. Sarah removed the clip from her trembling finger. She must have been dreaming of him, to have called out his name like that.

Not "harm me."

Harmon.

Harmon Smith, the man in the black hat.

CHAPTER THIRTEEN

"The goats is riled," Betsy Ward said.

She dried her hands on her apron, wincing because her skin was chapped and the cool weather hadn't helped a bit. She had a sweet potato pie in the oven. It was a point of pride with her, because sweet potatoes didn't grow worth a darn in the mountains. Yet Arvel's crop always turned out fine. You'd think God was a tater man, judging how He blessed the Ward household.

"Goats?" Arvel was watching a reality show on TV. Betsy couldn't tell the shows apart, but one thing they all had in common was they got the women into tank tops and tight shorts at some point. Which was all the reason Arvel needed, whether he admitted it or not.

Betsy's tight-shorts days passed some twenty years ago, but she didn't hold that against the skinny little things that paraded around before the cameras. No, what she held against them was the make-up, the hair styles, and all the nipping and tucking and padding that went on these days. Any woman could look good with a little cheating.

"Goats," Betsy said. "Over at the Smiths. Except the widow ain't named Smith."

Arvel put in a hard day at Drummond Construction, driving a concrete mixer over the twisting mountain roads. Concrete mixers were the most contrary vehicles on earth, according to Arvel. The weight could shift in two directions without warning, and once in a while the slooshing mix of sand, gravel and mortar coincided with the deepest cut of a sharp curve, and nothing offered a mortality rate like the rump-over-clutch-pedal tumble of twenty tons of cement and steel. Or so he said.

"What are you worrying about goats for?" Arvel didn't turn from the flickering light of the screen. "They've not got in the garden in two years or so. Leave them be."

"They ain't right. They come down to the edge of the fence and stare at me when I'm hanging out laundry."

"Maybe you ought to lose some of that fat ass of your'n and then they'd quit staring."

Arvel never made a mention of her weight until he'd taken up watching TV every weeknight, some five years back. Since then, he'd scarcely shut up about it. She wished she could shrink inside her gingham dress, but she was here and this was all of her. "They started up about time the new wife moved in. Been breeding like rabbits, too."

"You know how them billy bucks are," Arvel said. "They'll stick it in anything that wiggles, and some things that don't."

A commercial came on for some kind of erectile dysfunction product, and a wattle-necked old guy was in a hot tub with a woman young enough to be his daughter. Arvel thumbed down the sound with his remote. "You keep going on about the Smith widow. If you want to know what I think, I bet you're mad as a piss ant because she's skinnier than you."

Betsy was double upset. Arvel had no business checking out the neighbor's figure. Even though Betsy did, every chance she got.

"She ain't no skinnier than Gordon's first wife, and you never said a thing about her," Betsy said.

"Rebecca was different," Arvel said, eyes flicking back to the TV to make sure the commercials were still going and

Arvel was listening. "She's from here."

"She was," Betsy corrected. "*Was.*"

"Let's not get into that."

"She drove too fast for these twisty roads. Heck, Arvel, I know she turned a few heads, probably even yours, but the stone truth of it is she got what was coming to her."

"Like *you* know what happened to her?"

"I ain't saying a thing. The sheriff and the rescue team called it an accident, and they know better than me."

"Solom's took more than a few through the years," Arvel said. "It was her turn, that's all. Forget it."

"I *can't* forget it."

"You think it was the Horseback Preacher?"

"I don't know."

"But you know it was the preacher who took Gordon Smith, don't you? None of us swallowed that story about Gordon trying to murder the widow's first husband."

"Gordon was a good neighbor to us. Kept to himself and traded fair on the livestock. Speak nothing but good of the dead, God rest his soul."

"I sure to God *hope* he's resting. Enough dead things walking around Solom."

The commercials were over and Arvel punched a button. The sound burst from the speaker, and a dark-skinned boy with greasy hair was explaining why somebody was kicked off the show. "I smell something," Arvel said.

The pie. The crust must have burned. Betsy had forgotten to set the timer. She was getting more absent-minded every day, but she blamed it on worrying about the neighbors. With a possible husband-killer next door—assuming Betsy didn't buy into the legends—not to mention his witchy-eyed stepdaughter, your train of thought was liable to get derailed now and then. When you threw the Horseback Preacher into the mix, it's a wonder anybody in Solom ever got a wink of sleep.

She hurried from the living room and went into the kitchen, where the goat was waiting for her.

CHAPTER FOURTEEN

Evening fell like a bag of hammers, and Odus decided there was no better place to let the sun die on you than the cold bank of Blackburn River. Two rainbow trout waggled on the stringer and half a six-pack of Miller High Life floated in the water, the plastic ring tethered to a stick. The mosquitoes had quit biting weeks ago, and even if they were sorry enough to try to suck his blood, they would be drawing nothing but high-octane, eighty-six proof out of his veins. The bottle of Old Crow was nearly gone, and that meant another long haul into Windshake to replenish his supply. He cussed God and the Virgin Mary—and the high-minded, hypocritical voters— for making Jefferson a dry county.

He was below the old remnants of the dam. Part of the earthworks was still in place, funneling water past in a series of tiny falls. The trout loved to lie among the rocks beneath the white water, where the oxygen level was rich and food dropped down like earthworms from heaven. Odus's hook dropped in, too, although he had to work the reel with a steady hand because the bait washed downstream in the blink of an eye.

The general store up on the hill was dark. That was contrary, because Odus had never known it to be closed for a full day. He'd called up to the hospital to check on Sarah, and the receptionist hemmed and hawed about federal privacy rules until Odus claimed to be her son. Then the receptionist declared Sarah to be in stable condition and scheduled to be kept overnight for observation.

A few tracks from the old Virginia Creeper line, some that hadn't been washed away in the 1940 flood, lay in weed-infested gravel across the river. The creosote crossties had long since rotted, and the steel rails themselves would have been overgrown if the tourists hadn't made a walking trail out of the line.

Tourists were the damnedest creatures: they sought out the ugliest eyesores of Solom, such as fallen-down barns and lightning-scarred apple trees, and proclaimed them a glory of Creation. Took pictures and bought postcards, put their fat Florida asses onto the narrow seats of expensive ten-speeds, and pedaled down the river road as if they were going nowhere and had all day to do it.

Beat all, if you asked Odus, but nobody asked, because he was just a drunken river rat and didn't even own any property. He lived in the bottom floor of a summer house and kept the grounds in trade for rent.

But, by God, he knew how to troll for trout, and he could take a ten-point buck in November, and when spring came he could pick twelve kinds of native salad greens, and in summer he knew where the best ginseng could be poached, and then it was fall again and he could make a buck or two putting up hay or helping somebody get a few head of cattle to the stockyards. All in all, it was a king's life, and he wasn't beholden to anybody. If you didn't count the Pennsylvania couple that owned the house where he boarded, and the Smith widow, and the people who'd loaned him money.

The sun slipped a notch lower in the sky, spreading orange light across the ribbed clouds like marmalade on waffles. Fish often bit more at dusk, just as they did at the break of dawn, because the insects they fed on were more active then. A lot of the tourists went in for fly-fishing, and all the gear, complete with hip waders, LL Bean jacket, floppy hat, woven basket and all, would run you upwards of $300 at River Ventures. The little shop up the road rented out kayaks, canoes, bicycles, inner tubes, and every other useless means of transportation known to man. Odus figured the tourists must be bad at math, no matter how many zeroes they notched in their bank accounts, because $300 would buy you more grocery-store trout than you could eat in a year.

But that wasn't his worry. Odus wanted one more rainbow on the trotline before he headed home for a late supper. He planned on stopping by Lucas Eggers's cornfield on the way home and snagging a few roasting ears. That and some turnip greens he grew in the Pennsylvania folks' flower garden were plenty enough to keep the ache out of his belly.

He hit the Old Crow and was about to draw in one of the Millers for a chaser when he saw weeds moving on the far side of the river. The rusted-iron tops of the Joe Pye weed shook back and forth as something made its way to the water. Probably deer, because, like the fish, they got more active at sundown. But deer were likely to stick to a trail, not tromp on through briars and all.

Odus played out some slack in his line and waited to see what came out on the riverbank. Odus didn't have a gun, so he couldn't kill the deer, and so didn't care if it was a deer or a man from outer space. As long as it wasn't a state wildlife officer ready to write him up for fishing without a license.

At first, Odus thought it *was* a wildlife officer, because of the hat that bobbed among the tops of the weeds. But the hat was dirty and ragged like that of—

The Smith scarecrow?

Then the weeds parted at the edge of the river.

The sight caused him to drop his pole in the mud, back up onto the slick rocks skirting the riverbank, and wind between the hemlocks and black locust that separated the water from the river road. His heart jumped like a frog trapped in a bucket. The orange light of sunset had gone purple, and the clouds somehow seemed sharper and meaner.

A bright yellow light shone above the general store's front entrance, the one Sarah claimed kept bugs away, though Odus could see them cutting crazy circles around the bulb. He broke into a jog, sweating under his flabby breasts and in the crease where his belly lay quivering over his belt. He didn't once look back, and even though the river was between it and him, he didn't feel any safer when he reached his truck.

Odus was fumbling the key into the ignition when he remembered the Miller, and for just a moment, he hesitated. He would definitely need a good buzz later. But three beers wouldn't be nearly enough to wash away the image that kept floating before his eyes. The best thing now was to put some distance between him and what he'd seen. Maybe some tourist would be out for a walk, or a bicyclist would get a flat tire, and it could take them instead.

As he drove away, his chest was tight and he could barely breathe. He wondered if he could get a hospital bed in Sarah's room, because now he knew what she'd been going on about as she lay on the sacks with her eyelids fluttering.

It hadn't been the scarecrow he'd seen. It was much worse than that. The man in the black hat, face white as goat cheese, as if he'd been in the water way too long.

And he had, if you believed the stories.

About a hundred and fifty years too long.

CHAPTER FIFTEEN

"Did you hear something?" Jett asked.

"Nothing but a creaky old farmhouse doing a slow dance in the wind."

But Katy *had* heard it. It wasn't the settling and groaning of old wood. The sound was light and percussive. Like footsteps.

Above them.

They were sitting in the living room, Katy tapping away at her laptop, checking out her old Charlotte friends on Facebook. Jett was doing homework, or at least shoving enough papers around to make it look like she cared.

"If that's a goat up there, I'm not moving a muscle."

"Doors are locked," Katy said. Even though rural communities were supposedly safer than the big city, Katy had gotten back in the habit after Gordon had gone psycho. "Can't be a goat.

"Great. That means it's either Rebecca or the Horseback Preacher."

"Or maybe nothing."

"Mom, please. We can't both be experiencing the same auditory hallucinations. Unless you're taking acid without telling me."

"Drugs aren't a joking matter, especially after what they've done to our family."

"Jeez, Mom, lighten up. I thought getting attacked by a psycho hubby in a scarecrow outfit while being chased by an army of killer goats might have mellowed you out a little."

The percussive noise upstairs faded, and Katy realized Jett was trying to distract them both from fear. But both bedrooms were up there, and Katy didn't want to go up there after dark. Better to check it out now.

Or else plug your ears and go "La-la-la" and hope it goes away.

"All right," Katy said, setting her laptop on the coffee table. "You get your homework done. I'll take care of business."

Jett gleefully shoved her papers into her math textbook and slammed it shut. "Seriously. Remember your catchphrase? 'We'll get through it together.'"

"That doesn't work if we both get killed."

Jett headed for the stairs. "It's been a year. Things are about as normal as they're ever going to get."

Katy wasn't so sure. She hadn't see Rebecca's decapitated ghost since Gordon attacked them, but she'd seen wisps of movement out of the periphery of her vision from time to time. The headless scarecrow Gordon crafted as some sort of bizarre effigy of her still hung in the barn. Maybe Rebecca was just waiting for the right season to return.

Katy hurried to hit the first step before Jett, swinging out from the newel post to give her daughter a bump with her hip. They raced up the stairs, giggling like kindergarteners. They stopped when they reached the upstairs hall.

The closet door between their bedrooms was open.

"Were you in there?" Katy asked.

"Not lately. Nothing in there but towels and toilet paper."

And the attic access.

But the access must have been shut, because its folding ladder wasn't visible. Sunlight spilled from both of their bedrooms, erasing any gloom the old farmhouse might have imparted. Katy forced a laugh.

"Here we are, spooking ourselves over nothing," she said.

"I'm not afraid," Jett answered. "This beats the heck out of homework."

"Nice try, young lady." Katy wrapped an arm around Jett's shoulders and guided her back down the stairs. "Now get it finished so I can look it over before dinner."

"Like that would do any good. This math wasn't even invented when you were in the tenth grade."

"I'm not as dumb as I look."

"I'm not touching that one." Jett stomped back down the stairs, and Katy waited a moment before glancing into Jett's bedroom to verify it was empty, as well as the bathroom. She entered her own bedroom, the same one she'd shared with Gordon. She'd made him buy a new mattress when they'd married, but the antique four-poster bed was the same one in which he'd slept with Rebecca.

Katy should have bought a new bed, but with the uncertainty over the civil suit filed by Charlie Smith, she avoided needless expenditures. Her Charlotte friends, after venting their shock over Gordon's aberrant behavior, assumed she would sell out and move back as fast as possible. But part of her would have viewed that as a defeat, letting Gordon Smith's shadow fall over her even though he was in the grave. She had earned this farm and assumed more right to it than did any distant member of the Smith bloodline.

However, if Rebecca's spirit were still around, wouldn't it be fair to say it belonged to *her*? Hadn't she paid the ultimate price?

She glanced through the window at the cornfield, briefly reliving that horrible night when she and Jett had been attacked by Gordon, who wanted to spill their blood as a sacrifice to the Horseback Preacher. Gordon nearly killed Mark in the process, but the preacher rejected the offering and instead skewered Gordon with the long wooden pole that held the scarecrow. Katy liked to think the preacher's own violent death led him to choose the innocent over the depraved and profane.

Yeah, right, like any of us are innocent. Mark has a criminal record for drugs, Jett endured her own struggle with addiction, and I'm batting oh-for-two on choosing marital partners. And the only common denominator in all my failures is me.

Mark had called her that afternoon, ostensibly to discuss Jett's progress at school, but he'd probed into personal territory as well. She'd drawn away as politely as she could — after all, they still needed to raise a child together — but she'd found herself thinking of him more and more often these days.

She glanced at the bed. Desperation. She hadn't been intimate with anyone in more than a year, and sex with Gordon had been distant and strange. Mark was a winner in that arena, but no way was she going to weaken now.

I have to set a good example for Jett. You always move forward.

As she was leaving the room, she noticed the silver mirror and hairbrush on the vanity. The mirror handle was tarnished gray, a Smith heirloom. She was sure she'd packed it away in the attic with the other objects she associated with Gordon. But she knew to whom the mirror and brush belonged.

Rebecca.

Katy picked up the mirror and looked into its fogged glass. The reflection looking back almost startled her — her red hair was lush and full, but her face was haggard, as sharp as the blade of an ax. Dark wedges curved under each eye, and creases etched the corners of her mouth. Her freckled skin was grainy.

Crap, I'm starting to look like a scarecrow myself.

She slid open a vanity drawer and placed the mirror and hairbrush inside.

"Okay, Rebecca," she whispered. "I guess we can share the house. Just don't borrow my sweaters without asking first."

CHAPTER SIXTEEN

Betsy Ward didn't scream when she encountered the goat. She'd milked plenty of the critters, and the teats were tiny and tough, a workout for her hands. But they usually kept to the field, even when they were riled. Occasionally one slipped through a gap in the fence or squeezed between two gate posts, but when they did that, they usually made a beeline for the garden or the flower beds. Goats had a nose for heading where they could do the most damage.

But she'd never had one come in the house before. The back door was ajar, as if the goat had nudged it open with its nose. The mesh on the screen door was ripped. Maybe the goat planted one sharp hoof on the wire and sliced it down the middle. Goats weren't that smart, even if they smelled something good in the kitchen.

In this case, the only thing going was the sweet potato pie. No doubt the goat smelled that and came in for a closer look, though Betsy had no idea how in the world the creature had worked the door knob. Why hadn't Digger run the goat off, or at least raised the alarm with his deep barks?

"Shoo," she said, waving her apron at it. "Get on back the way you come."

The goat stared at her as if she were a carrot with a spinach top.

"Arvel," Betsy called, trying not to raise her voice too much. Arvel didn't like her hollering from the kitchen. He thought that amounted to pestering and henpecking. Arvel said a wife should come up to the man where he was sitting and talk to him like a human being instead of woofing at him like an old bitch hound.

"Arvel?"

Arvel must not have heard her over the television. The goat's nostrils wiggled as they sniffed the air. The oven was a Kenmore Hotpoint, the second of the marriage. In the red glow of the heating element, she could see the pie through the glass window in the oven door. The surface bubbled a little and the orange filling was oozing over the crust in one spot.

The goat lowered its head and took two steps toward the oven. It sported small stumps of horns and was probably a yearling. Sometimes a goat would get ornery and butt you, but in general they avoided interaction with humans, except when food was at stake. It seemed this goat had its heart set on that sweet potato pie.

Betsy shooed with her apron again, then scooted so she was standing between the oven and the goat. She didn't think the goat could figure out how to work the oven door, but some sense of propriety overtook her. After all, this was her kitchen. "Get along now."

The goat regarded her, eyes cold and strange. She didn't like the look of them. They had the usual hunger that was bred into the goat all the way back to Eden, but behind that was something sinister. Like the goat had a mean streak and was waiting for the right excuse.

"Arvel!" By now Betsy didn't care if her husband thought she was henpecking or not. You don't have a goat walk into your kitchen and expect to take it in stride. She'd gone through a miscarriage, the blizzard of 1960, the drought of 1989, and the flood of 2004.

She knew hard times, and she knew how to keep a clear head. But those things were different. Those were natural disasters, and this one seemed a little *unnatural*. Like maybe the goat had something more in mind than just ruining a decent homemade pie.

Betsy stuck her hands out, hoping to calm the animal, but its cloven hooves thundered across the vinyl flooring as it rapidly closed the ten feet separating them. Betsy saw twin images of herself reflected in the goat's vertical pupils. Her mouth was open, and she may have been screaming. Her hair hung in wild, slick ropes around her face. She didn't have time to step away even if she could have made her legs move.

The goat hit her low, its head just above her womanly region, driving into her abdomen. The nubs of the horns pierced her like fat, dull nails, not sharp enough to penetrate but packing plenty of hurt. The unexpected force of the assault threw her off-balance, and she felt herself falling backward.

The kitchen ceiling spun crazily for half a heartbeat, and she saw the flickering fluorescent light, the copper bottoms of pans arranged on pegs over the sink, the swirling patterns in the gypsum finish above.

Then she was falling and the world exploded in sparks, and she thought maybe the pie filling had leaked onto the element. As she slid into the inky, charred darkness, the smell of warm sweet potatoes settled around her like the breath of a well-fed baby.

"Pie's done," she whispered. Her eyelids fluttered and then fell still.

CHAPTER SEVENTEEN

Odus eased his truck into the gravel lot of Solom Free Will Baptist Church, parking beside the Ford F-150 driven by the Rev. Mose Eldreth. Most likely the preacher was taking on an inside chore, mending a loose rail or patching the metal flue that carried away smoke from the wood stove. A dim glow leaked from the open door, framing the church's windows against the night sky. Odus cast an uneasy glance in the direction of Harmon Smith's grave, but the white marker looked no different from the others that gleamed under the starlight.

Odus didn't hold much stock with Free Will preachers, but at least Preacher Mose was local. Preacher Mose knew the area history and, like most of the people who grew up in Solom, he'd heard about Harmon Smith. After all, Harmon owned a headstone in the Free Will cemetery. That didn't mean the preacher would talk to Odus about it. Like Sarah Jeffers, most people in these parts didn't want to know too much about the past.

Odus went up the steps and knocked on the door. "You in, Preacher?"

A scraping sound died away and there was the metallic echo of a tool being placed on the floor. "Come in," Preacher Mose said.

It was the first time Odus had been in a church in a couple of years. He'd attended the Free Will church in his youth, but the congregation didn't think much of his drinking so he'd been shunned out. He didn't carry a grudge. He figured they had their principals and he had his, and on Judgment Day maybe him and the Lord would sit down and crack the seal on some of the finest single-malt Scotch that heaven had to offer. Then Odus could lay out his pitch, and the Lord could take it or leave it.

Although hopefully not until the bottle was dry.

The Primitives were different, though. A little drink here and there didn't matter to them, because the saved were born that way and the blessed would stay blessed no matter how awful they acted. Odus could almost see attending that type of church, but he liked to sleep late on Sundays. As for the True Lighters, they took religion like a whore took sex: five times a day whether you needed it or not.

Preacher Mose was kneeling before the crude pulpit up front. He wasn't praying, though; he was laying baseboard molding along the little riser that housed the pulpit and the piano. A hand drill, miter saw, hammer, and finish nails were scattered around the preacher like sacraments about to be piled on an altar. Preacher Mose was wearing green overalls, and sweat caused his unseemly long hair to cling to his forehead. "Well, if it isn't Brother Hampton."

"Sorry to barge in," Odus said. "I wouldn't bother you if it wasn't important."

"You're welcome here any time. Even on a Sunday, if you ever want to sit through one of my sermons."

"Need a hand? I got some tools in the truck."

"We can't afford to pay. Why do you think they let me carpenter? I'm better at running my mouth than running a saw."

The church was without electricity, and even in the weak glow of a battery-powered spotlight propped on the seat of a front pew, Odus could tell the preacher's baseboard joints were almost wide enough to tuck a thumb between. "This one's on the house. A little love offering."

"Know him by his fruits and not by his words," Preacher Mose said.

"Good, because my words wouldn't fill the back page of a dictionary and half of those ain't fit for a house of worship."

Odus retrieved his tool kit from the bed of the pick-up and showed the preacher how to use a coping saw to cut a dovetail joint. After the preacher nicked his knuckles a couple of times, he got the hang of it and left Odus to run the miter saw and tape measure.

The preacher bore holes with the hand drill so the wood wouldn't split, then blew the fine sawdust away. "So what's troubling you?"

"Harmon Smith."

The preacher sat back on his haunches. "You don't need to worry about Harmon Smith. His soul's gone on to the reward and what's left of his bones are out there in the yard."

"That's not the way the stories have it."

"I'm a man of faith, Odus. You might say I believe in the supernatural, because God certainly is above all we see and feel and touch. But I don't believe in any sort of ghost but the Holy Ghost."

"Do you believe what you see?"

"I'm a man of faith."

"Guess that settles that." Odus laid out an eight-foot strip of molding, saw that it was a smidge too long. "Always cut long because you can always take off more, but you sure can't grow it back once it's gone."

"I'll remember that. Maybe I can work it into a sermon." Preacher Mose drove a nail with steady strokes, then took the nail set and sunk the head into the wood so the hole could be puttied.

"What I'm trying to get around to is, I seen him."

"Seen who?"

"Harmon Smith."

The preacher paused halfway through the second nail. Then he spoke, each word falling between a hammer stroke. "Sure" —*bang*—"don't" —*bang*—"know" —*bang*— "what ... "—*bang*. He paused, then wound up with a flourish. "...in heaven's name you're talking about" —*bang bang bang BANG*.

"He come down by the river while I was fishing. Face like goat's cheese and eyes as dark as the back end of a rat hole. He had on that same preachin' hat you see in the pictures."

Preacher Mose drilled another hole and positioned the nail. Odus noticed his hands were shaking.

"Sarah Jeffers saw him, too, only she won't own up to it."

The preacher swallowed hard and swung at the nail. The hammer glanced off the nail head and cut a half-moon scar in the wood.

"A little putty will hide it," Odus said. "That's the mark of a good carpenter. It's all in the final job."

Preacher Mose swung the hammer again, the head glancing off his thumb this time. "God duh—" He stuffed his thumb in his mouth and sucked it before he could finish the profanity.

"Don't be so nervous. It's just a finish nail."

"Harmon Smith died of illness. He caught a fever running a mission trip to Parson's Ford. He had a flock to tend, and his sheep were scattered over two hundred square miles of rocky slopes."

"That's the way the history books tell it. But some people say different, especially in Solom."

"And they probably say there's a grudge between us and the Primitives."

"No, they don't say that."

"We all serve the same Lord, and on the Lord's Earth, the

dead don't walk. Not 'til Rapture, anyway."

"Maybe you ought to tell that to him." Odus lifted his hammer and pointed the handle to the church door. Framed in silhouette was the tall, gangly preacher, the one who was nearly a hundred and fifty years dead.

Preacher Mose knelt at the foot of the pulpit and stared at the black-suited revenant. He put his bruised thumb back in his mouth and tightened his grip on the hammer until his knuckles were white.

Harmon Smith's shadow moved into the church and up the aisle.

But before Odus could live a hammer, the revenant vanished.

CHAPTER EIGHTEEN

When Arvel heard the noise from the kitchen, his first reaction was annoyance, because one of the guys on TV was about to get voted off the show. It was the guy with the bandanna who hadn't shaved; there was one on every reality show. Arvel could always tell which asshole was going to get cut loose, although it never happened in the first few episodes.

No, they had to string the audience along and let all the viewers build up a real hate for the guy, which was made worse by the fact that he just might have a chance of winning. Which would mean another asshole millionaire in the world while folks like Arvel still got up at six a.m. and put in ten hard hours. Well, only seven if he could help it.

So he'd been working up a decent dose of spite for the asshole in the bandanna when the floor shook and thunder boomed in the kitchen, like his wife had dropped four sacks of corn meal. But since she couldn't lift even *one* sack of corn meal, it meant something else had dropped.

His wife, all hundred and ninety-five pounds of her.

His first thought when he entered the kitchen was: *Damn, she's burnt the pie.*

Then he saw his wife sprawled on the kitchen floor and forced himself to remain calm. He'd been a volunteer firefighter for over a decade, ever since a liquored-up cousin set one of his outbuildings on fire by dropping a cigarette in a crate of greasy auto parts. Arvel didn't know all the fancy techniques used by the Rescue Squad folks, but he'd watched them in action plenty of times.

His favorite emergency tech was Henrietta Bannister, who was built like a cross between Arnold Schwarzenegger and Julia Roberts, except unfortunately Henrietta had Arnie's chin and hairline and the Pretty Woman's nose and muscle tone. Despite this unsettling mix, she was cool as a September salamander when the pressure was on, and it was her voice that Arvel now heard in his head. He repeated the imagined lines to his wife as he knelt beside her and felt for her pulse.

"Hey, honey, looks like you had you a little mishap"— *check your pulse, don't know a damned thing about how fast it's supposed to be, maybe it's MINE that's thumping like a rat trapped in a bucket, but yours feels mighty shallow—*"but don't you worry none cause old Arvel's right here beside you. We'll get through this and have you baking lemon cakes again in no time."

Arvel put a cheek near her lips, making sure she was still breathing. He looked at the back door, where he'd seen the flicker of movement as he'd entered the room. He was almost sure it was some kind of animal, and he was getting ready for a closer look when he saw Betsy laid out like Sly Stallone in *Rocky*, only Sly managed to climb up the ropes and lose on his feet while Betsy appeared down for the count.

She was still drawing air, but her eyes were hollow and sunken. He lifted one eyelid, just the way Henrietta would do. Betsy's pupil was as tight as a BB. Her long skirt bunched around her knees, revealing a purple road map of varicose veins. Arvel felt the back of her head and found a raised place the size of a banty-hen egg.

"You just got a little concussion, is all," Henrietta would say. She spoke in that slow, reassuring way even when the patients were unconscious. Once Arvel heard her waltz a car-crash victim through death's door with that same soothing kind of talk.

Arvel didn't think he could pretend to be Henrietta anymore, because he wondered what would happen if his wife stopped breathing. "Don't die on me, now," he said, a line Henrietta would never use in a hundred years. "I can't afford to be alone. Not when I need more warm bodies between me and the Horseback Preacher."

What if it was HIM that come calling? What if those pounding noises were made by horse hooves?

He went for the phone and dialed 9-1-1 with no problem, and then found himself talking to the communications officer in Henrietta's words. "Is this Francine?"

Of course it was Francine, because Arvel knew all the communications folks from the scanner he kept in his truck. When Francine said, "Yes, go ahead," Arvel took a deep breath and said, "Sorry to bother you, but I was wondering if you could have the squad come down to 12 Hogwood Road in Solom. I've got a patient down."

"What's the emergency, sir?"

"I'm not no sir. I'm Henrietta. I mean, this is Arvel Ward." Somewhere in his glove box was a sheet with all the emergency response codes, but since his job was putting out fires or occasionally directing traffic, he'd never bothered to memorize the list. All he knew was that, in car wrecks, "PI" meant "personal injury" and "PD" meant "property damage," and you hurried with the red light and siren for the first of those but not the second. So he said, "We got a PI here, weak pulse, possible head injury. Plus something's burning in the oven."

"Hold on, Arvel, we'll get somebody right there. Are you with the patient?"

"Not right now. I'm on the phone."

"I meant, is the patient in the house with you?"

"Yeah. She lives here."

"Okay, stay on the phone and let me give you some instructions."

"I can't leave her alone, and the cord won't reach. Tell them to hurry, and send Henrietta."

Arvel hung up. When he got back to the kitchen, he knelt over her again to check her pulse. His fingers touched a wet place on the floor. He lifted his hand and saw it was blood, leaking from somewhere just above her waist.

Arvel wondered if maybe Betsy had landed on a butcher knife when she fell, because it surely wasn't her head giving off that much blood. He tried to roll her over but she was too heavy. Finally, he lifted her enough to see a rip in her dress and the burgundy maw of a wound in her side, a few inches below her rib cage. It looked like some kind of bite mark, because the edges of the wound were stringy and jagged.

He looked once more at the back door, wondering what kind of beast had wandered in and taken a chunk out of his wife. And wondering why Digger hadn't raised holy hell, and whether Henrietta would know how to handle something like this.

Because, right now, with Henrietta's voice in his head or not, he couldn't think of a single comforting thing to say.

CHAPTER NINETEEN

Sue Norwood turned around the sign in her window to inform any late-night cyclists that she was "Closed—Gone Fishing." Not that she'd ever cared for sport fishing, even though she sold Orvis rods and reels, hip waders, hand-tied flies, coolers, Henry Fonda hats, and everything the genteel fisherman needed except for alcohol.

Solom was unincorporated, which precluded a vote on local alcohol sales, and Sue figured in maybe five years the seasonal homeowners from Florida would own enough property to push for a referendum. For now, she was content to bide her time on that front. The pickings were easy enough as it was and the dollars trickled in, much of it in cash.

In 1999, Sue purchased a little outbuilding that belonged to the Little Tennessee Railroad, one of the few structures in Solom to survive the 1940 flood. It sat within spitting distance of the Blackburn River, but was on ground just high enough to survive the calamities that Solom seemed to call down upon itself. Ice storms and blizzards were biannual events, high water hit every spring and fall, hellacious thunderstorms rumbled in from March through July, and the winter wind rattled the siding boards like they were the bones of a scarecrow.

But all the outbuilding needed was a green coat of paint, a $20,000 commercial loan at Clinton-era rates, and sixty hours of Sue's time each week to hang in there despite Solom's lack of a true business climate.

Sue converted an upstairs storage room into an apartment,

and it was to this space she retired after closing. She passed the racks of kayaks that stood like whales' ribs on each side of the aisle, making sure the back door was locked. As an all-season outfitter, she'd packed the place with every profitable item she could order, from North Face sleeping bags to compasses to Coleman gas stoves. Ten-speed bicycles were lined against the front wall, with rentals bringing in more than enough to keep her wheels greased.

Ever since Lance Armstrong trained along the old river road before his third run at the Tour de France (a little factoid that Sue always managed to slip into her advertising copy, when she couldn't get the local media to mention it for free), out-of-shape amateurs had been flocking to the area to rest their sweaty cracks on her bicycle seats.

At $30 a day, they could hump it all they wanted. She was even willing to sponsor a community fundraising ride for the Red Cross each summer, a nice little tax write-off that paid back in spades.

Sue counted the bikes before she went upstairs, her last official chore for the day. Two were still out. She checked her registration records at the desk and found the bikes were rented by a Mr. and Mrs. Elliott Everhart of White Plains, New York. Fellow Yankees. Sue was from Connecticut herself, but she'd graduated from the University of Georgia with a degree in exercise science followed by three extra years in Athens as an assistant coach for the women's field hockey team, pretty much flattening her vowels and slowing down her speech enough to pass for Southern if she were drunk.

At the age of 25, she'd written down the names of all her favorite rock-climbing spots, clipped them apart with scissors, and randomly pulled one out of a hat. Solom wasn't on the list, but it had been the closest to the Pisgah National Forest, which featured Table Rock and Wiseman's View. Solom was near a river, and rock-climbing wasn't exactly a major source of commercial recreation income, since it required little more than a rock and an attitude. So she'd launched River Ventures and expanded ever since. Funny thing was, she'd been so busy these past few years with her business that she rarely saw the sun herself.

The Everharts.

Sue could remember them because the husband, Elliott, detected her up-coast accent and remarked upon it. Sue couldn't remember the wife's name, but she was a quiet, willowy blonde who spoke little and didn't seem all that thrilled with the idea of human-powered transportation. They rented the bikes at 2 p.m. and estimated their return at 6 p.m.

Elliott told her they'd rented a cabin on the hill above Solom General Store and had walked down so as not to take up a parking space in the small gravel lot. Sue had said, "Thank you kindly," an artificial Southern response that had come more and more easily over the years, then sent the couple on their way with bottled mineral water—respectably marked up to $2 a pint—and a map.

Sue checked the clock above the front door, the one that elicited native bird calls with each stroke of the hour. It was ten minutes away from Verio, nearly two hours later than the Everharts' anticipated return of Crow.

People who rented bicycles sometimes got flats. It was rare, because she kept the equipment well maintained. All those who rented gear, whether it was a propane lantern or a kayak or a ten-speed, were required to sign release forms absolving River Ventures of any responsibility. That didn't mean people didn't screw up, especially the types of deep-pocketed but shallow-skulled clients to which Sue usually catered. Even if the Everharts had gotten lost or suffered a breakdown, they most likely could have walked back to

Solom, flagged a ride, or called for assistance on their cell phones.

Except Sue could see three problems with that scenario, because she'd experienced each of them. Sometimes bikers got lost when they tried to walk back, since the going was so much slower that the maps became deceptive. Flagging a ride was no guarantee because there simply wasn't that much traffic after sundown in Solom, and outsiders were loath to pick up anyone wearing fluorescent Spandex and alien-looking crash helmets. And cell phones were almost universally useless in Solom because the valleys were deep and the old families owning the high mountains had yet to lease space for transmitting towers.

Sue considered a fourth alternative. The Everharts appeared to be in their thirties and were presumably childless, at least for the length of their vacation. Maybe good old Elliott had gotten a boner for nature and coaxed his wife into the weeds for a little of world's oldest and greatest recreational sport. Or maybe the willowy blonde was the one to turn into a ravening maw of wild lust.

As far as Sue could tell, there was no reason to call out the search-and-rescue team just yet. Besides, she earned an extra $30 for late fees and the Everharts had placed a $500 deposit on their credit cards to cover much of the value of the bikes. With depreciation, subsequent tax write-off, and the tip they'd probably give when they rolled in red-faced tomorrow morning, Sue figured the old saying "Better late than never" wasn't quite as good as "Better late and *then* never."

She left on a small light above the desk, went up the stairs at the back of the store, and made herself a dinner of canned salmon, creamed rice, and fresh collard greens, all heated over a Coleman gas stove. The stove was a legitimate business expense. She'd checked with her accountant boyfriend,

Walter, whom she'd met on a whitewater rafting expedition.

Though the relationship launched on Class-Four rapids, it had drifted into shallow eddies by summer's end. That was okay, too. The money she'd spent on condoms and Korbel champagne were a valid tax write-off. Sue anticipated a warm meal ahead and a vibrator waiting under her pillow, the famous Wascally Wabbit that was never too "hare-triggered" and didn't lie or cheat.

If the Everharts came knocking in the middle of the night, she planned to sleep right through it.

CHAPTER TWENTY

Elliott was being a total dick.

Carolyn Everhart didn't like to think of her husband in such bald, crude terms, but he'd taken the whole vacation as a measure of his testosterone levels. From booking the rental car to deciding on restaurant stops on the trip down, Elliott always had a snappy answer for her every question, and a good reason why he knew best. As they'd followed the Appalachian foothills south, Elliott seemed to have grown wax in his ears and a fur pelt that hadn't graced humans since they'd started shaking their Neanderthal origins.

They'd picked Solom almost at random. Elliott worked at PAMCO Engineering with a guy who'd attended Westridge University and said the North Carolina Mountains were relatively unspoiled ("A perfect place to get away from it all while still having it all").

An Internet search and credit card reservation later, and they were booked in the Happy Hollow retreat for a week, and since October was leaf season, the cabins cost a premium. A two-day drive from White Plains, with a Holiday Inn Express layover ("Complete with a 'lay,' what do you think, honey?") in Scranton, Pennsylvania, and they had arrived with not a single argument over road maps.

But here in the failing light, she couldn't get Elliott to even look at the map, much less admit they were lost. The pocket map they'd picked up from the outfitters' was fine as long as they stuck to the river road, which was flat and gently curving. But Elliott insisted on what he called "a little off-roading," though after two hours her legs had begun to cramp and the air temperature dipped into the low 40s.

Instead of complaining, she pointed out that the bikes were geared for road racing and not mountain climbing. Too late. The name "Switchback Trail" had intrigued him. Besides, he'd complimented her on how the biking shorts snugged her ass, and that bought him a little slack.

Elliott chased down a forest trail barely wide enough for a fox run, and that trail branched off twice, crossed a narrow creek, and cut around a cluster of granite boulders that rose like a backwoods Stonehenge from the swells of the earth. Two forks later ("The road less traveled or the road not taken, what do you say, you liberal arts major, you?") and he'd juddered over a root in the gathering darkness and been thrown over the handlebars. No bones broken, but some serious scrapes that would require antibiotic ointment.

Now they stood in a cluster of hardwood trees whose branches were nearly devoid of foliage. If any houses were around, their lights didn't show. Small, unseen animals skirled up leaves around them and darkness was falling harder and faster than a philandering politician's poll numbers. Carolyn, a homemaker, Humane Society volunteer, and member of the Sands Creek subdivision bridge club, resisted the urge to say "Well, we really got away from it all, didn't we?"

Elliott pulled a pen light from his fanny pack and played it over the bicycle. "I think the front wheel's warped. We'll have to pay for the damage when we get back."

"You mean 'if' we get back."

"I know exactly where we are."

"Show me, then." She pulled out her copy of the fourfold pocket map. It was bordered with ads for area tourist attractions, fine dining establishments, and investment realtors. The river road was marked by a series of arrows, and the Solom General Store and River Ventures were represented by red X marks. State highway 292 leading from Windshake was clearly delineated in thick black ink. Tester Community Park, about five miles from the outfitters' judging from the scale of the map, was the last recognizable landmark they'd passed.

"We're right about here," Elliott said, running the beam over the pen light in a printed area that represented two square miles.

"There aren't any lines there," Carolyn pointed out.

"Sure. But we were headed east, remember? The sun was sinking behind us."

Actually, Carolyn recalled only vague glimpses of the sun once they'd left the relatively familiar flatness of the pavement. What bits of scattered light did break through the gnarled and scaly branches seemed to originate from a different position with each new slope or fork.

When the sun had settled on the rim of the mountains, the entire sky took on the shade of a bruised plum, and Carolyn was thinking by then that even a trail of bread crumbs out of "Hansel and Gretel" wouldn't have led them back before midnight.

"Can the bike roll?" she asked.

"Sure, honey." Elliott lifted the bike by its handlebars and spun the wheel with one hand. The wheel made three revolutions, the rubber sloughing erratically against the tines, before it came to a complete stop. "Well, it can work in an emergency."

"At what point does this become an emergency?"

"Take it easy, Carolyn. We can walk out of here in no time. Once we find the river, we'll be home free."

"Do you know where the river is?"

"Sure, honey." He took the map from her and fixed the pen light on the place he'd decided was their present location, despite having zero evidence. With the beam, he traced a line to Blackburn River on the map, which was conveniently marked with a sinuous swathe of blue. "We're here and the river's there. A half-hour's hike, tops."

"I see the river on the map, but where's the river out here?" Her voice took on the tiniest bit of sarcasm despite her best efforts.

"Water runs downhill. Ergo, we walk downhill, and there will be the river."

"Ergo" was one of those annoying, know-it-all, engineering-type words Elliott occasionally sprang on her when he was feeling defensive.

"I'm glad we wore athletic shoes and not moccasins," Carolyn said. Elliott had stopped at a little souvenir stand when they crossed the North Carolina border, one with a fake moonshine still by the front door and a wooden bear sculpted with a chainsaw. She'd talked him out of buying the Rebel flag window decal and the Aunt Jemima figurine-and-syrup-decanter ("Just wait till the guys at PAMCO get a load of these authentic tastes of the South!"), but he'd gone for the genuine hand-stitched leather Cherokee moccasins at $29.95 a pair.

"Do you have any water left?" He'd used up the last of his water rinsing his wounds.

"A little," she said. Though she was under no illusions that they'd be back in the comfort of their rental cabin within the hour, she didn't think they were at the point where they'd need to conserve water to survive. She handed him her bottle and he dashed some in his mouth and swallowed.

"Okay, let's rock and roll," he said, walking his bike back down the hill. Just enough daylight remained to reveal the darker cut of the trail against the thick tangles of low-lying rhododendron. She tucked the map in the tight pocket of her biking shorts and followed, the bike leaning against her hip.

They had gone fifteen minutes before the invisible sun slipped down whatever horizon led to morning on another side of the world. Elliott switched on the pen light and its weak glimmer barely made a dent against the walls of the forest.

"Remember those big rocks we passed?" Carolyn asked, the first time she'd spoken since they'd started their descent.

"Yeah."

"We should have come to them by now."

"They're probably uphill from us. We're at a lower elevation now."

"'Probably'?"

He flicked the beam vaguely to his right. "Sure, honey. Up there. We'll come to that creek soon, and then we can decide whether to follow it down to the river or stick with the trail."

It was the first time he'd hinted that any decision would be mutual. That should have given her a cheap glow of victory, but it actually made her more nervous than she wanted to admit. She looked behind her, hoping to recognize the trail from their earlier passage, but all she could see were hickory and oak trees, which stood like witches with multiple deranged arms.

"Let's hurry," she said. "I'm getting cold."

The colorful nylon biking outfits gave a pleasant squeeze to the physique, but they were designed to let the skin breathe so sweat could dry. Breathing worked both ways, though, and the soft wind that came on with dusk made intimate entry through the material.

"I think I remember this stand of pines," her husband said. He gripped the pen light against one of the handlebars as he walked, so the circle of light bobbed ahead of them like on one of those "Follow the bouncing ball" sing-a-long songs on television. Carolyn thought the perfect tune for their situation would be AC/DC's "Highway To Hell."

It was maybe a minute later, though time was rapidly losing its meaning during the interminable trek, that Carolyn heard the sounds behind her. At first she assumed they were the echo of her footsteps, or maybe a whisper generated from the bike's sprockets. She breathed lightly through her mouth, or as lightly as she could, given the fact that she was bone tired, a little bit pissed, and more than a little scared. Leaves rustled. Something was moving, larger than squirrel-sized, churning up dead loam and breaking branches.

She edged her bike closer to Elliott's until her front tire hit his rear.

"Jesus, Carolyn. Are you trying to run me down?"

"I heard something."

"I hear lots of somethings. Didn't you read the guidebook? The Southern Appalachians are home to a number of nocturnal creatures. Don't worry, all of the large predators are extinct, thanks to European settlers. Ergo, nothing to fear."

"Can we stop and listen for a minute?"

"Every minute we stop is another minute we're lost."

"I thought we weren't lost."

"We're not. We're just reorienting with our intended destination."

"Try the cell phone again?"

"No bars. Signal's deader than Bobby Kennedy."

Ten minutes later and they reached the creek. The gurgling of the water and the cold, moist air alerted them to its presence before they blundered into it, because the pen light's beam had begun to fade. Carolyn welcomed the discovery not because it was the first definite landmark—if, in fact, it was the same creek as they'd crossed earlier—but because the white noise of the rushing water masked the sounds of the footsteps that followed their tracks a short distance behind.

"The creek, just like I said." Elliott pointed the light into Carolyn's face. It was barely bright enough to make her squint. "The question is, do we follow the water or stick with the trail?"

Carolyn was tempted to remark that he was finally asking her opinion, now that the situation had reached the south side of hopeless. Instead, she allowed him to retain a sliver of his pride. After all, there *would* be a later, and the politics of marriage, just like the politics of a republic, were constantly swinging from one party to another. And the pendulum was going to be weighted to her side big time for the rest of the vacation.

People didn't wander off and die in the Appalachian Mountains. There was just too much development. Maybe in Yellowstone, where grizzly bears still roamed, or the Arctic Wildlife Refuge with its sudden snow storms and sub-zero temperatures. Here, the worst that could happen was a miserable night in the woods, with granola bars for supper and a surly husband to endure.

Except something had been following them. No matter what Elliott said.

"We shouldn't trace the creek," she said. "It looks like the rhododendron get thick down there, and all those rocks are probably slippery. One of us might fall and break an ankle, then we'd be in real trouble."

"Good point."

Another blow for girl power, but Carolyn didn't think the creek was that dangerous. She was afraid she wouldn't be able to hear the footsteps over the rushing water. "Why don't we leave the bikes here? We can't ride them, and they're slowing us down."

"We paid a deposit."

"We can come back and get them tomorrow, once we figure out where we are."

"I know where we are. I'm an engineer, remember?"

"Ergo." Carolyn didn't mean for the response to sound so bitter, but she was cold, her rump was sore from the ten-speed's narrow seat, her calves ached, and her face and arms were scratched by branches. "In case you haven't noticed, this isn't a problem you can solve with quadratic equations."

Elliott's widened eyes doubly reflected the pen light, as if she had slapped his face. She savored the victory for a mere second and decided to finish the coup. She grabbed the light from his hand and swept the beam against the surrounding trees and underbrush, like Luke Skywalker slashing down Empire storm troopers.

"I heard something out there following us, and I'm good and goddamned scared." She hadn't used two expletives in the same conversation since her days at Brown, and it gave her a sense of what the feminists called "empowerment." It was frightening. She would give up power for security any day. But she had a feeling she needed the adrenaline and anger if she was going to get them out of this mess.

"Okay, okay, calm down," Elliott said, and the patronizing tone was suppressed but audible. "You're right. We should leave the bikes and stick with the trail. Let's cross here and hide the bikes in that thicket, then keep walking."

"Fine." She trembled, and she didn't know whether it was from the chill mist of the creek or her anxiety. She held the light while Elliott guided his damaged bike through the water, carefully choosing his steps on the mossy stones so his shoes would stay dry. He slogged through the mushy black mud of the opposite bank and stood above her, lost in the dark web of wood and vines.

"Come on, Carolyn. I can't see anything."

She took one look behind her, half expecting to see a crazed black bear or a red wolf or even a mountain lion, then navigated the rocks and headed up the embankment. She slipped once, going to one knee in the lizard-smelling mud, but Elliott grabbed her upper arm and tugged her to solid ground. Then he dragged the bike up and wheeled it into the bushes.

"Do you want to have a snack?" he asked. "An energy bar or something?"

"I want to get out of here."

"Let's look at the map one more time."

Carolyn nodded and gave the pen light back to her husband. She recognized that she had literally and figuratively passed the torch, but she didn't care. Truth be told, she was nearly in tears. So much for her run as Margaret Thatcher or the Republican Hillary Clinton.

They moved a little away from the water and gathered around the pen light as if it were a battery-powered campfire. Somewhere above them, the moon had risen, but its reassuring glow was filtered into teasing gauze by the treetops. Elliott was studying the map when Carolyn heard the scrape and rustle of leaves.

"Did you hear that?" she asked, her heart a wooden knot in her chest.

"Just the wind. Or maybe a raccoon."

"The wind's not blowing. And raccoons don't get that big." Carolyn was struck by the image of a mutant, man-sized raccoon, reared up on its hind legs, crazed yellow eyes blazing from a bandit mask. The image should have made her chuckle, at least on the inside. Instead, the tension increased its grip on her internal organs. And, goddamn, she suddenly needed to pee.

She didn't relish peeling down her nylon shorts and squatting in the darkness, further exposing herself to whatever was out there.

"Okay, if we're right here and can make three miles an hour, we should reach the main road by eleven o'clock. Then we can find a house and call for a cab or something."

The idea of walking up on a stranger's porch and knocking was almost as scary as the thing that was or wasn't following them. "I don't think they have cabs out here."

"Maybe the police. Or the Happy Hollow office."

Elliott must be scared, too. Otherwise, he'd never admit to others that he'd made a mistake. Carolyn's knowledge of his failure was one thing, he could gloss that over in the coming week and eventually have her believe getting lost had somehow been *her* fault.

But here he was ready to tell the local sheriff's department or the rental cabin management that he'd wandered off with no respect for the wilderness, that his modern-day James Fennimore Cooper act had gone bust, that a Yankee engineer with a wristwatch calculator couldn't navigate the ancient hills. Carolyn couldn't wait, even if it meant he'd be pissy until they made it back to White Plains.

Mostly, she couldn't wait to see a street light.

Because the noise was back, closer, to the right now.

"You heard *that*?"

"No." He said it so firmly it sounded like self-denial.

"It's closer."

His face contorted in the dying orange orb of light. "Listen, Carolyn. This is the twenty-first century, not the goddamned 'Blair Witch Project.' In real life, people don't get stalked by cannibalistic hillbillies or eaten by wild animals. And, last I heard, aliens don't have secret landing sites in the

Appalachians. That's the Southwest desert, remember? Ergo, there is nothing following us and I'm trying to solve this little problem you created and get us safely back to civilization."

Leaves rustled ten feet ahead of them, behind a gnarled evergreen. Despite herself, Carolyn moved closer to Elliott and clung to his arm. He stiffened and smirked.

"I'll get us out of here," he said. "Have I ever let you—"

The pen light died and darkness rushed in like water flooding a ruptured bathysphere. It was almost as if the light warded off the other sounds of the night, because the still air was filled with chirring, scratching, and creaking. Beneath those came the ragged whisper of breathing.

Carolyn's eyes adjusted to the dim moonlight just in time to see a large black shadow hover beyond Elliott, then her husband was ripped from her grasp. He gave a wet gurgle, as if a freshet had erupted between the granite stones of his face. One of his legs flailed out and struck her kneecap, and he gave a bleat of pain. Drops of liquid spattered on Carolyn and she screamed.

The air stirred above her head and she looked up to see a curved and dripping grin of metal catch the distant eye of the moon. The grin descended and bit with a meaty *thunk*, and all Carolyn could think was that the meat must have been her husband, that arrogant engineer with a fondness for college football, the Bush clan, plasma television, and pharmaceutical stocks.

The scream jumped the wires from her brain to the ganglia low in her spinal cord, a place encoded during the Paleozoic Era when flight meant survival and the higher thinking processes shut their useless yammerings.

She ran blindly, branches tearing at her hair, heedless of the trail's direction. The moist hacking continued behind her, but she scarcely heard, because her eardrums protected her high-order brain. She was an animal, scrambling through the leaves, guided by instinct as she ducked under branches and dodged between scaly oaks and beech.

She couldn't see but she didn't need to see, because her eyes were jiggling orbs of dead weight in her skull and a more primitive sight led her onward. All knowledge was in her skin, mind given over to flesh, she was aware of nothing but the roar of wind through her throat and the pulse in her temples and the dark sharp thing at her back and—

She didn't see the maple with the low branch, because her eyes shut down, but she did see the bright yellow and green sparks that exploded like fireworks on the movie screen of her forehead.

Carolyn was unconscious as the goats gathered around her, and her useless, high-order brain stayed mercifully absent as her true-blue Republican blood leaked into the land of legends.

CHAPTER TWENTY-ONE

The general store was crowded with a mix of locals and tourists. Odus, his ball cap tipped low and a toothpick between his teeth, stood by the sandwich counter and waited as Sarah rang up the purchases of a chubby boy in too-tight nylon biking shorts and tank top. The customer's shoulders were pink and peeling, the sign of a spoiled city boy getting too much sun on vacation.

The boy's dad stood beside him in a red sweat suit that was meant to portray athleticism, but instead gave the impression of a sausage that was about to bust out of its skin. Sarah bagged the boy's mound of candy bars, pork rinds, and lollipops.

A bluegrass band was tuning up in the park across the road. A Solom community group bought four acres along the river that was now cleared and grassed, with a band shell at one end. From early summer until the end of October, weekly shows were held in the park. The music was either bluegrass or traditional old-timey, though the general store hosted occasional debates about the difference between the two labels. Odus plucked some mandolin himself, and even sat in on some local recording sessions, but he didn't like performing in front of people.

Sarah looked away from the register and frowned at him. He gave a small nod that said, "We need to talk after you take care of business."

Sarah paid rapt attention to the customers, smiling as if she appreciated them for more than just their money. A six-pack of Mountain Dew, two cups of overpriced coffee, a microwave burrito, a honey bun, a bottle of sun block, a rustic bird house, a basket made of entwined jack vine, a stack of Doc Watson CD's, and two bags of Twizzlers changed hands before Sarah got a break. She picked up a dusting cloth, came to the sandwich counter, and began wiping down the dewy glass.

"You had me worried," he said.

"Don't waste a good worry on me."

Normally Odus wouldn't. Sarah Jeffers was tougher than beef jerky and had the backbone of a mountain lion. But toughness and spine didn't matter when you were standing up against something that ought not be. Odus ground the end of his toothpick to splinters as he spoke around it. "I seen him."

"Seen who?" Sarah said, suddenly taking a great interest in the chub of gray liverwurst. Odus didn't see how anybody could eat that stuff. Bologna was okay, but he preferred good and honest meat, like ham, that looked the way it did when it came from the animal.

"We both know who," he said.

A tan, Florida-thin blond approached the cash register, pigtails tied with pink ribbons. She wore a T-shirt that read "THIS DOG DON'T HUNT." In her hands were a gaudy dried flower arrangement and a miniature wooden church, no doubt decorations for a seasonal second home. Sarah's face relaxed in relief as she went to ring up the sale.

"Are you the storyteller?" a voice behind him asked.

He turned and faced a man wearing sunglasses who held a cassette tape as if filming a commercial. Odus was on the cover, dressed in his folksy garb of denim overalls and checked flannel shirt. He'd even borrowed a ragged-edged straw hat for the photo because the university woman who recorded it said the package needed what she called a "hook." Odus didn't know a damned thing about marketing, but he knew stories from eight generations back.

The Hampton family had passed along the Jack tales, in which Jack usually put one over on the old King. "Jack and the Beanstalk" was the best-known of the stories, but that one didn't have a king in it. The university woman said they were parables in which the Scots-Irish who settled the Southern Appalachians were able to get proxy revenge on their English oppressors. Odus didn't feel particularly oppressed by anybody in England, except maybe when Princess Diana got all that attention for getting killed, but he figured the university woman was a lot smarter than he was about such things.

"I did some telling on that one," Odus said. The tape was called "The Mouth of the Mountain."

"So you're a celebrity." The man was eating a Nutty Buddy ice cream cone and a string of white melt rolled down the back of his hand. He licked it up.

"Not really. I just talked. The woman who made the tape did all the work." Odus looked over at Sarah, who was busy taking money for a gee haw whimmy-diddle, a folk toy that basically consisted of three sticks and a tiny nail. Retail value: $6.99 plus tax.

"Do you tell them in public? We're going to be up for two weeks and would love to hear some authentic Appalachian stories."

"They ain't authentic," Odus said. "They're all lies."

The man laughed, ejecting a tiny peanut crumble that arced to the floor at Odus's feet. "That's good. I'm buying this one, and I'm sure I'll be pleased. If you're not holding any performances, can I hire you to come down and tell some stories around the campfire in our backyard?"

Sweat pooled in Odus's armpits. He didn't mind telling the stories to family or his few close friends, and he could even put up with talking them into a microphone, but the idea of spinning out some Jack yarns while a bunch of tourists yucked it up and sipped martinis was more than he could stand. "I don't do tellings in a crowd," Odus said.

"This won't be a crowd. Just us and the neighbors. Maybe ten people."

"Ten's a crowd."

The man looked at the tape. "Fifteen dollars for this, huh? I'll pay a hundred dollars for one hour."

Odus thought of the wallet in his back pocket, the leather folds so bare a fiddleback spider wouldn't hide in them. A hundred bucks would buy a case of decent whiskey, and decent whiskey would maybe drown out those dreams of the cheese-faced man in the black hat. From the park, the sounds of the string band blared from the PA speakers. "Fox on the Run," complete with three-part harmony.

The man was mouthing the waffle cone now, running his thick, pink tongue around the cone's rim.

"I'll have to think on it a spell."

The sunglasses hid the man's expression, which could have been disbelief or impatience. Odus didn't much care. It wasn't like losing a steady job or anything. If he'd even wanted a steady job, that was.

"I'll listen to the tape and get back to you," the man said. "What's the best way to reach you?"

Odus took the toothpick from his mouth and pressed the tip into his callused thumb. "I don't have no phone. Usually you can find me here at the store or around."

The man smiled, vanilla cream on his upper lip. "Okay, 'Mouth of the Mountain.' Have it your way."

He paid for the cassette and left the store. Odus watched

through the screen door as the man made his way to the park.

"Sold a tape," Sarah said. "There's another buck-fifty for you."

"Except I don't get it for six more months," Odus said. "That royalty thing."

Sarah took a five out of the cash register and held it out to him. "I'll report that one as damaged. Call it an advance."

Odus swallowed hard and went to the counter. The store was quiet. An elderly couple was browsing in the knick-knacks and a kid faced tough choices at the candy rack. Odus reached out and took the bill, but as he pulled his hand away, Sarah grabbed his wrist with all the strength of a possum's jaws.

"Take it and buy you a bottle, and forget about it," Sarah said. "You ain't seen nothing, and I ain't seen nothing."

Their eyes met. Odus, at six feet two and 240, somehow seemed to be looking up at Sarah, who stood all of five feet and weighed in at a hundred soaking wet. "He's back, and getting drunk won't change that."

"Getting drunk never changed anything, but that never stopped you before." Sarah let go of his wrist. "Don't go blabbing it or people will think your brain finally pickled and they'll throw you in the ward at Crazeville to dry out."

"The people I tell it to will believe me, because they'll know."

"I heard what you told that man. Your stories ain't authentic, they're lies." Sarah began fussing with the cigarette packs and cans of smokeless tobacco behind the counter.

"The biggest lies are the easiest to swallow," Odus said. "But they burn like hell when you puke them back up."

He went out into the sunshine and the last chorus of "Fox on the Run."

CHAPTER TWENTY-TWO

Carnivorous goats.

Sounded sketchy to Alex Eakins, even from the isolated fantasyland of his libertarian paradise. He could dig zombies, even cheer for them in a way, because when you got down to it, those brainless gut-munchers from beyond the grave were about the most libertarian creatures around. Talk about your free-market economies. But goats were another matter.

Alex was smart enough to be aware of his eccentric nature. His parents were afraid he was turning into a survivalist who would one day construct an armed bunker and have a stand-off with federal agents. But the true survivalist didn't want to be noticed by the government, much less stage a confrontation. And a true survivalist didn't go around ranting about man-eating goats, because that was a sure-fire way to get noticed.

So Alex would have to figure out how to handle this on his own. The first order of business was a trip to the general store to get a few reels of barbed wire. He could add another couple of runs around the perimeter of his property as a first line of defense. His gun rack held a .30-.30, a 16-gauge Remington shotgun, and a .22 so his girlfriends could participate in target practice.

He carried his bow and arrows, a slingshot, and a couple of sticks of dynamite he'd bought under the table at the last Great Tennessee Border Gun Show. Plus there was the contraband arsenal in his secret room. So goats, even a herd of them, were not something to lose sleep over.

Weird Dude Walking was another story altogether.

Because Alex had returned to the scene of the slaughter and found that not even a stitch of clothing remained. No blood on the ground, either, and not a goat in sight (the Remington was with him just in case). Goats would eat any old thing, especially natural-fiber clothing, but surely a few scraps would be scattered around, or a bone button from the coat. Strangest of all, though the ground was pocked with cloven hoof prints, there was not a single mark from the man's boots.

Which meant Weird Dude Walking must have risen up and floated away like Christ gone to heaven.

Even if Alex wanted to report what he'd witnessed, he had no evidence. He never doubted his sanity, although his own family had called him "wacko" any number of times. But only a wacko would witness a man feeding himself alive to a bunch of goats.

Maybe not wacko, though.

Maybe special.

If a thing like that happened in the old days, the people called you a prophet and let you boss them around. The thin line between messiah and lunatic.

"Alex?"

Meredith. Alex looked up, not realizing he'd been staring at his palms as if expecting them to start bleeding. "I thought you were at work."

"It's my day off."

"Oh yeah."

"Something wrong?"

"No, babe. Just thinking about the state of the world. It's a guy thing."

"I've got a guy thing for you." Meredith nuzzled her breasts against his back and put her arms around his chest.

"Not now. I've got some things to work out."

"Don't you want to smoke some?"

"I need to keep a clear head. Dope is the opium of the masses."

"Huh?"

"Hemingway. He said dope is the opium of the masses. But that's pretty fried, because opium is what they make heroin out of, and not many people can hook up with some 'H.' I guess they didn't smoke much weed back in Hemingway's time."

"I thought he said *religion* was the opium of the masses."

"Same thing. Religion is for dopes, so it all works out." He gave a stoned snicker, though he'd not smoked any marijuana since the night before. He was more or less riding a chronic buzz these days.

"You want some lunch? I could cook one of your acorn squashes and some wild rice."

"I'm not hungry. I think I'll go check the babies and meditate."

He got up from the table and went outside. He owned a small greenhouse, but he didn't grow his dope in it. The surveillance planes might see it and that would be the first place the snooper troopers would train their little spy cameras. His marijuana was in a little shed by the garden.

He used a wind turbine and water wheel to generate electricity for the full-spectrum lights, because one of the ways cops got a warrant was by checking the electric company's records for a jump in kilowatt hours. The jump was "evidence" that a citizen might be using grow lights. Since he was off-grid, he was outside the system, in more ways than one.

He unlocked the shed, checked the sky for bogies, and went in. The main room was filled with a blue glow thrown off by the bank of grow lights. Marijuana plants, spawned from Kona Gold seeds a friend mailed from Hawaii by way of Tucson, stood as tall as Alex, and the room was sweet with the fully flowering buds. The three dozen plants were grown in five-gallon buckets, and the soil was ripe with the best compost Mother Nature could produce. Alex sat cross-legged before the plants in a yoga position. He was at peace in this place, this shrine to the sacred buzz.

Too bad he had to hide it away. In a righteous world, he could grow it out there in the garden, right in front of God and everybody. Even Weird Dude Walking. If grass were legal, maybe the country's farmers wouldn't need crop subsidies. Get them off welfare and stifle the Fed's war on drugs at the same time. Damn, why couldn't the Libertarians come up with any good candidates?

Well, he knew why. True libertarians were like Taoists, they couldn't exist in nature. They were snakes swallowing their own tails in an endless loop, defeated by their own inherent contradictions.

He let his anger at social injustices slip away as he breathed deeply of the *cannabis sativa*. A spider had spun a web at the base of one of the plants. The spider was yellow with black streaks across its back, and it worked its way toward the center of the web where a struggling fly was tangled in the silken threads.

Alex realized the display was life in a microcosm, a symbolic play. You buzz around minding your own business, and then suddenly your ass is snared and along comes Reality to suck out your juices.

Just like the goats sucked the life out of the man in the black hat.
Heavy.

Too heavy to contemplate with a straight head, despite what he'd told Meredith. He just didn't want to smoke with her, because then he'd either have to talk or else silence her in bed. The only way to shut up a woman was to stick part of yourself in her, sometimes even your heart. He needed to be alone. He pulled a joint out of his sock and fired it up, not shifting from his yoga seating as he puffed. He began a game of situation-problem-solution.

Situation: You had a vision. Nobody else will believe you, because you don't belong to any religion of the masses. Well, Meredith will probably believe you, but she believes in Atlantis and UFOs and even the Great Pumpkin.

Problem: You either keep it to yourself and forget it, or you have to admit that miracles happen. And that you were specifically chosen to witness one.

Solution: Smoke more dope.

He took a deep draw off the joint and held the smoke in his lungs. In his mind's eye, the blue smoke seeped into his blood stream and sent its tendrils into his brain. The drug stimulated him and relaxed him at the same time, one of its contradictions that appealed to him and suited his worldview.

Been a long time since you were in Methodist Bible School, but miracles in the Bible sort of had a point to them. Like Jesus with the loaves and fishes so everybody could eat, and Jesus turning water into wine so everybody could get wasted. Far as I can remember, nowhere in the Bible did some dude feed his own ass to the goats. But there's your precedent.

Alex took another puff. The spider finally reached the fly, which must have worn itself out, because it stopped struggling. Or maybe the fly had sensed the jig was up and could see two dozen copies of the approaching spider through its compound eyes. Alex considered rescuing the fly, playing God, releasing it to go off toward it appointed tasks of eating shit and hatching maggots.

But it wasn't right to fuck with Nature. Besides, that

would have meant standing up, and his legs had a nice tingle going.

Situation: Weird Dude Walking had to come from somewhere. Miracles don't just crawl down off the top of the mountain in the middle of the Blue Ridge, half a world away from the Red Sea and Egypt and Jerusalem.

Problem: That means Weird Dude was an emissary of some sort. Sent by God or the devil or what the movie trailers called the 'dark imagination of M. Night Shyamalan.' An emissary sent specifically for YOU, Alexander Lane Eakins, and for you alone.

Solution: Just because an emissary drags ass to your castle door doesn't mean you have to open up and let him in. Pretend it never happened. Denial is A Good Thing.

The joint was down to an orange roach, and Alex hot-boxed it until it burned his fingertips. He exhaled the smoke so that a blue cloud swept over the spider and the fly. One could get the munchies and the other could die with a shit-eating grin. Seemed to be some sort of circular cosmic justice in that.

He sat until the sparkling edges of his buzz wore off, then he went into the house to ignore Meredith.

CHAPTER TWENTY-THREE

Sue Norwood spent the morning doing inventory.

Winter was not a big merchandise season in Solom, and the kayak rentals all but died as the weather got colder. She normally took December off, though she'd thought about starting up a cross-country skiing racket and see if she could get the Floridians to bite. Trouble was, most of them took off at the first frost. Besides, the end of the year was a time to start lining up tax deductions.

Today she'd only served three customers: a scruffy college kid who purchased a North Face sleeping bag, a housewife who popped in for a two-dollar tube of Wounded Warrior all-purpose healing salve, and Kim Deister, a local blond with a flat tire on her ten-speed. Sue noted that the Everharts hadn't turned in their rental bikes during the night.

She was patching a split seam in a kayak with fiberglass and epoxy when the bell over the door rang. She figured it was the Everharts, limping in sore and tired. "Hello?" she called from her work area in the corner of the shop.

"Miss Norwood?"

"Odus? Come on back, I've got mess on my hands."

Odus Hampton wasn't really a regular, although he occasionally bought some fishing hooks or monofilament line. She sometimes hired him for heavy lifting if big shipments came in, and he was happy to work for store credit. He taught her a lot about the river, and she'd taken him out in a canoe a few times so he could show her the currents, falls, and rough patches.

She'd offered to hire him as a river guide, but he wasn't interested in steady work, though he'd filled in a few times when Sue was under the weather. She trusted his outdoor experience, partly because he camped out for most of the summer, even though he did it on the cheap, without a Coleman lantern, mosquito netting, or a pair of steel-toed Herman Survivor boots.

"Busted a boat?" Odus said. "You ain't been crazy enough to take that out on the river? The water's probably forty degrees."

"I'm getting it ready for spring. This is the only time I have to catch up. Did you go fishing today?"

Odus shook his head, his full beard brushing the tops of his overalls. "The fish won't be biting."

"I thought they always bit for you." The fumes from the epoxy were giving her a headache.

"Not when the water's tainted."

"What's wrong with the water? Did it get contaminated?" The Blackburn River was designated a national scenic river, and President Clinton had even given a speech there. No factories or major commercial farms lay along its banks, and the headwaters sluiced down from largely undeveloped mountains. If Sue suspected problems with water quality, she'd have screamed for Greenpeace, the Southern Environmental Defense League, the local branch of the Democrat Party, such as it was, and the North Carolina Department of Environment and Natural Resources.

Clean water was money, just like scenic beauty was money. A lot of mountain communities were selling out their slopes to millionaires who built garish houses with too many lights. Change was inevitable, but Sue wasn't going to let Solom go to hell until she was ready to retire.

"It ain't what's *in* the water. It's what's *got* the water,"

Odus said.

"Don't scrunch up your eyes that way. Makes me worry."

"Maybe you ought to."

"Oh, the legend thing. The kind of tall tales you tell for money."

"You're not from Solom, so you won't understand."

"I'm as much a part of this place as I'll ever be."

"All right, then." Odus's eyes roamed over the store and settled on the bike rack. "You got two bikes out."

"Yeah, a couple rented them yesterday and hasn't turned them back in yet. I figure they pulled a few muscles and are lying in bed trying to recuperate."

"Where were they going?"

"They didn't say, but they headed east up the river road."

"I think I'll run my truck up that way and have a look."

"Do I need to call them? They left their cell phone number on the deposit slip."

"It's probably nothing. Just some odd goings-on got me a little spooked."

Sue looked up the number and punched it in on her phone. A monotone female voice came on the line and informed her that service to the number was unavailable. "This valley's got more dead spots than a cemetery," Sue said.

"You got that right," Odus said. "If you see any strangers, keep a close eye on them."

"I like strangers. They usually have money in their pockets."

"Not the one I'm talking about."

"Damn it, Odus, why do you have to be so mysterious? Why don't you just come out and say it?"

"Because you'll think I'm drunk. Or worse."

Sue nodded in agreement. "You got me on that one."

"We're having a meeting at the general store after closing

time. Come over and you'll find out more than you want to know."

"Sure. It's not like I got anything better to do."

Odus ignored her sarcasm. *Dang, maybe this is serious. Can't even get a grin out of him.*

"I'll come by to pick you up at eight," he said. "I'll need you to come with me. There's a stop we got to make before the meeting, and it might need a woman's touch."

Sue looked at her fingers, wondering exactly what kind of touch he was talking about it.

"Are you part of Solom or not?" he asked.

She nodded.

Sue followed Odus to his truck, checking out the river where it made a gentle bend below the store. She'd built a small ramp leading into the water to serve as a launch for canoes and kayaks. A patch of brambles, stalks of Joe Pye weed, and tangled pokeweed stirred along the riverbank. The yellowed vegetation parted, and a goat's head emerged. The animal's horns caught the autumn afternoon light and gleamed like a couple of bad teeth.

"Hell of a lot of goats around here lately," Odus said through his open window. The engine wheezed to diseased life, throwing a clot of blue smoke into the air.

"Should I call the police about the cyclists?"

"Solom likes to take care of its own."

That's the trouble, Sue thought, as Odus guided the truck down the road between the post office and general store.

CHAPTER TWENTY-FOUR

Sarah Jeffers watched Odus drive by in his Blazer, gritting her dentures.

Why did he have to stir things up? Just like a Hampton. Back in her father's day, a branch of the Hamptons operated a grist mill and feed store on the back side of the mountain. When the state paved the roads in the 1930s, people found it was easier to drive into Titusville and buy their corn meal and flour rather than pay to have their own crops ground. The general store lost some business as well, but her father expanded with the times, going for cigars, candy, and pulp magazines.

The Hamptons stuck to tradition and tradition left them busted. The grist mill still stood by a silver creek, like the bones of a dinosaur that had died standing up and was too dumb to fall over. The Hamptons retreated back up into the hills, selling off their land, and generally ending up like Odus, either drunk or living hand-to-mouth.

Sarah changed with the times, too, and times lately had gone deep into the contrary. She convinced herself she hadn't seen the Horseback Preacher, but Odus wouldn't let her hold on to that pleasant deception. And Gordon Smith's latest widow had been in today, buying the oddest assortment of goods the shelves could conjure. The last person to shop so impulsively was Gordon's first wife, Rebecca, that pretty, black-haired gal with dimples.

Rebecca was magic in the kitchen, and every fundraiser in the park or volunteer fire department pot luck brought out a few of her finest offerings. It was a terrible tragedy for her to run off the road like that. The emergency responders stopped in the next day for Dr. Peppers and a pack of Camels and told Sarah all the gruesome details. The car rolled, and Rebecca's head had been sliced clean off, her body bruised as if she'd been beaten with hammers. It was a closed-casket funeral. Sarah thought at the time the Jews had it right by burying their dead on the same day, the better to get it over with and move on.

Of course, after the Gordon Smith tragedy of last year, tongues wagged, and half the town was quick to blame the Horseback Preacher. Some even went so far as to call it revenge for Rebecca's death. People just liked Rebecca that much. Angels shouldn't die, but Sarah figured it was selfish of folks to want to keep them here on Earth.

A stack of cans fell over in the back corner of the store. It was the area where she kept the number 10 cans of vegetables, product that moved so slowly the cans often grew flecks of rust before someone bought them. She grabbed the broom, determined to addle the brains of any mouse that might be causing trouble. The store was empty of customers, not that unusual for mid-morning.

She moved past the black metal woodstove in the center of the store and through a few mismatched tables where the lunch crowd could enjoy their deli sandwiches. A sprinkle of black spots appeared before her eyes, but she told herself she wouldn't pass out again. She'd rather go down with a stroke than have Odus Hampton haul her to the hospital again.

Shelves on each side of her were packed with jelly jars, mountain crafts, floral arrangements, mass-produced folk art, motor oil, ropes, boxes of cookies, assorted screws, Thanksgiving table settings, dinner candles, rubber gloves, and mouse traps. She figured her store was as general as they came, and she held to a pet theory that customers were more apt to buy things they didn't want if they had to hunt hard for the things they did.

She turned the corner between the Coca-Cola cooler and a rack of picture postcards and came face-to-face with a goat. It must have been a wether—a castrated male—because she hadn't smelled it. Billies with balls liked to piss all over themselves when they were in rut, and they didn't smell too good any other time, either.

She'd never owned goats, though she sold stakes, chains, and collars for people who liked to use the animals as cheap lawnmowers. Sarah didn't have any particular grudge against goats, but she didn't want one messing around in her store leaving doodies the size of ball bearings.

"How did you get in here, you knot-head?" she said. Good question, one the goat didn't answer. The back door was locked and Sarah had been standing by the front door for at least the last half hour.

"Bet you belong to a Ward or a Buchanan," she said. "Nobody else would be sorry enough to let their critters roam wild."

The goat's mouth worked in that peculiar sideways twist, and Sarah looked around to see if it had chewed into any of the bird-seed sacks. The floor was clean, but the nanny goat was busy cudding up *something*. Sarah knelt and peered, not trusting her ancient eyes. She owned glasses but always left them by the register. Red specks dotted the animal's lips, and a pink strand of drool ran down the crusty beard.

"I can't tell what you're eating, but it damn well better not be my pickled beets." Sarah swept the broom around and gently swatted the goat on the shoulder. "Now get on out of here."

The goat continued chewing as if relishing a handful of

artichoke hearts soaked in molasses. Avoiding the curled horns, Sarah moved beside the animal and slammed the straw end of the broom against the goat's rump. The nanny looked at her out of its nearest eye, and Sarah saw a small version of herself in the rectangular slit of its pupil. The reflection looked scared.

"Get on, get on," she said, her voice nearly breaking. Because now something was crunching inside the animal's mouth like peanut shells. She delivered one more blow, and the goat took a few steps down the aisle, hooves scruffing over the hardwood floor. It looked back at her and seemed to grin before it headed to the front of the store, pushed open the door with its horns, and sauntered off the porch.

Odus had scheduled a little meeting here tonight to discuss the strange carryings-on, and Sarah wondered if she would tell what she'd just seen. Dangling between the goat's ochre teeth was a dark, wet string that looked for all the world like a mouse's tail.

CHAPTER TWENTY-FIVE

Alex surveyed the perimeter from the small glass windows along the front of his house. All clear for now, and Meredith was waiting tables on the night shift at the Ruby Tuesday's in Titusville. He finally took time to ponder his encounter of the day before, not distracted by her silly needs.

Goats as government conspiracy. It finally made sense to Alex. That's just how *they* would do it, come at him in the most unpredictable way possible. If only he had an Internet connection, he could go into some of the freedom organization chat rooms and learn from the fighters on the front lines. The government was tapped into every web server in the country, and in big underground caverns near Washington, D.C., NSA agents sat before banks of computers, monitoring every e-mail and phone record, surfing for people like Alex.

The enemy within.

If the government was behind the whole thing, then the man in the black suit must be some sort of genetic freak, the result of a secret experiment gone wrong. The fact that he was prowling near the Eakins compound meant only thing: *they* were on to him.

Four years of tax evasion wasn't that serious of a crime, not when Congress was busy stealing billions, but it was the principle of the thing. They didn't care about the money, they just didn't want word to get out that the government could be cheated and was therefore vulnerable. What better way to catch your enemy off guard than to come disguised as a backwoods preacher?

Except this preacher had been eaten alive. Even if he was an FBI agent in disguise, such a stunt took some effort. Maybe *they* used some sort of hologram. Classic brainwashing technique involved challenging the subject's notion of reality and eventually replacing reality with the desired set of beliefs. Alex nodded to himself, finished twisting a pinkie-sized joint, and lit up. He liked that answer better. Sure, he was paranoid, and like any free-thinking man, he had good reason. But he wasn't crazy.

With the joint hanging from lips *a la* Bogart in "Casablanca," he made his way to the back room, a space barely larger than a walk-in closet. He unlocked the two Case dead bolts and entered, searching for the candles he kept on an overhead shelf. Lighting one, he stood before his shrine: a wall covered with small arms firepower.

His pride and joy was an AKR submachine gun, a favorite deadly toy of the Russian special forces that held 160 rounds. Alex traded four pounds of seedless buds for the short-barreled gun, worth about eight grand on the street. The lethal and compact grace of the gun appealed to him as much as its country of origin. Not that the Russians could be trusted, either, but at least they were less cunning in their oppression.

Then there was the Swiss SIG 510 assault rifle. The good old Swiss claimed neutrality, but during every war of note, the country served as a clearinghouse for whatever loot happened to be pillaged by the victor. The Swiss made their weapons with all the love and precision they invested in their watches and chocolate. With bayonet, the rifle made a nasty but sleek package.

A row of well-polished handguns were spread across a velvet-covered shelf. A Mauser C-96 was the centerpiece. No hidden arsenal was complete without a piece of German hardware. It was an older model, manufactured between the two World Wars, but it possessed a heft and sheen that justified its place in the collection, though he'd only been able to procure two ten-round clips for it. The Germans were arguably the most militaristic people in modern history, except perhaps for the Japanese, Montana freedom fighters, and Republican presidents.

He owned an Austrian-made Glock, a weapon currently in favor with police officers, although he preferred the proven accuracy of the Colt Python. Occasionally, Americans mustered up some pride in their craftsmanship, and the Colt had pedigree. The Beretta resulted from a sense of romanticism only, because he'd never bet his life on something Italian, unless it was manicotti or a young Sophia Loren.

He owned a few other sidearms, a couple of M-1 practice grenades a staff sergeant smuggled out of Ft. Bragg, and a Mossberg 20-gauge shotgun. The collection also included the Pearson Freedom bow, which retailed at around $600, unless you happened to be swapping grass for it. As for arrows, he went with Easton, mostly because he'd known a kid named Easton growing up in Chapel Hill. An array of knives completed the collection, though they were mostly for show. Alex wouldn't have invested in all that hardware if he was interested in hand-to-hand combat.

The other walls of the room held posters, anti-establishment stuff, an Abbie Hoffman portrait, psychedelic posters of nothing in particular, an art print of Che Guevara, the Cuban revolutionary who was as famous for his beret as for his celebrity death photos. Richard Nixon, the patron saint of all latter-day paranoiacs, glowered down with his sharp nose and sinister eyebrows.

As he had in the well-lighted shed where his marijuana grew, Alex sat cross-legged before the wall that held his weapons. He sucked the joint down until it burned his lower lip, then he pinched it out and swallowed the roach. You couldn't leave evidence lying around, not when *they* might be closing in.

He shut his eyes and enjoyed the silence, the Python cool in his lap.

When the government agents came, he'd be ready.

CHAPTER TWENTY-SIX

The headlights swept up the driveway just as Katy was thinking about going to bed. She'd been dreading turning out the lights and laying there in the dark, listening to every little rustle and scrape while imagining Rebecca was prowling the house.

It was one thing to make peace with the notion of a spirit in your house, but it was another thing to accept the presence as normal. She hadn't mentioned the mirror and hairbrush to Jett. No need for both of them to be jumpy and sleep restlessly if at all.

The vehicle bobbing up the rutted gravel road was a welcome distraction, even though she never had uninvited guests. She recognized the raggedy muffler noise, though. It was from Odus Hampton's old truck.

Jett called from the top of the stairs, wearing her hopelessly uncool Hello Kitty pajamas. "What's Odus doing here this time of night?"

"I'll take care of it," Katy said, tugging her plaid flannel nightgown around her and heading for the door. "You go on and get to bed."

Outside, the night was beautiful, the crisp, cool air causing the countless stars to twinkle overhead. A goat gave an annoyed bleat from the interior of the barn. Frost already sparkled on the grass, and Katy's breath tumbled from her mouth in silver clouds.

"Hello, Miss Katy," Odus said, climbing out of the truck with a squeak of shock absorbers. "Sorry to barge in on you like this, but it's important."

"Who's that with you?"

"Sue from the outfitters' shop there by the river."

Katy didn't know Sue well, but she and Jett had once rented kayaks from her. Like Katy, Sue was an outsider who carved out a place in Solom. Another stray seed that had stuck and grown roots. "We were just getting ready for bed."

"Turning in early for a Saturday night," Odus observed, approaching the porch with Sue behind him.

"Country life. You know how it is."

"Sorry to barge in," Sue said. "I wanted to call first, but Odus said we needed to make this a personal visit."

"Because you'd hang up otherwise," Odus said. He glanced up to the lighted windows of the second floor and Katy wondered if Jett was watching.

"Okay," Katy said, standing to one side and waving them onto the porch. "I guess we're supposed to be neighborly now that we've settled here."

Sue gave a look of apology as she passed, but Odus smoldered with some sort of anger and enough whiskey fumes that she hoped his teeth didn't throw off any sparks. She settled them around the kitchen table and was about to ask if they wanted anything to drink, but she knew what Odus's answer would be.

"I hate to drag you into this," Odus said, "but the Horseback Preacher has come back around."

Katy glanced at the cupboard where she'd occasionally felt Rebecca's spirit, then out the window to the barn where a certain family scarecrow hung from a wire. "I'm afraid I don't know what you're talking about."

"You don't have to play the ignorant city slicker," Sue said. "Half the town believes it was Harmon Smith that attacked you and your daughter and killed Gordon."

"That's silly. Harmon Smith died a long time ago."

"Gordon was real big on his scarecrow legend," Odus said. "But he had an even bigger love for his ancestor's legend. I never pressed you on it, but I know there was more to that night than what they put in the police report. Sheriff Aldridge likes to keep things buried. Keeps him in office and saves the retirees from worrying too much."

"Sure, I've heard the legends, but—"

"He's back, Miss Katy. I didn't see him last time but I saw him yesterday, down by the river."

The lies fell out of her mouth so fast that she almost believed them herself. "Lots of locals wear old-fashioned clothes. That's more likely than a dead preacher coming back from the grave to seek revenge on Solom."

"Sarah Jeffers saw him, too," Sue said.

"I love Sarah to death, but she doesn't exactly possess what I'd consider the soundest of minds—"

"Mom," Jett said, coming in from the hall. Katy wondered how long she'd been standing there listening. Long enough, apparently. "Let's not bullshit anymore. If these guys know something, we should listen. The Horseback Preacher killed Gordon, but he could have easily killed both of us. Dad, too."

"That's the thing," Odus said. "He only takes one. But it's usually about once a decade. Now he's back at the same time of year as last year, like he wasn't happy with his harvest."

Katy put a protective arm around Jett's shoulders. "What does it have to do with us?"

"The last kill was here on your farm. You're in it whether you want to be or not. Hell, you might even *be* the next kill." Odus nodded at Jett. "Or your daughter."

That remark caused Katy to squeeze Jett even harder, but she ducked out of Katy's grip. "Okay, so he's back," Jett said. "What do we do about it?"

Katy knew she should have been more accepting. The supernatural was part of her life now. But she's obsessed over the things she could control—raising Jett, keeping ownership of the farm, maintaining a civil parental relationship with Mark.

But which of those DO you control? Are any of them more predictable than when the next Killer Goat Army rolls in with Harmon Smith leading the charge?

"Well, killing him is out," Odus said. "That's been done before and it didn't stick too well."

"What, then?" Katy blurted. "Make a creepy wax doll with a silly black hat and stick pins in it? Sacrifice a goat under the full moon? Recite Bible verses backwards to send him back to hell?"

"We're meeting on it down at the general store tonight," Sue said. "That's why we came. We figured your...*experience*...could help us."

"Is this really happening?" Katy asked.

"We're part of Solom whether we want to be or not," Jett said. "You made that choice for us. Now you have to live with it."

"Or die with it," Odus added.

"Maybe we'll be safer just sitting here and waiting it out," Katy said.

"Except for one other thing. Harmon Smith's victims always come back."

Katy's rib cage squeezed her heart with frozen ropes. "Gordon?"

"Could be."

"Jesus, Mom," Jett said. "No way am I waiting around for your Freddie Krueger ex in a scarecrow mask to come chop us up from beyond the grave."

Katy sighed. "Okay. Let me get dressed."

"Maybe we should call Dad," Jett said. "He's in on this, too."

Katy spun with a suddenness that startled them all. "No way. We can't drag him any deeper into this."

"I've worked with him and he's a good man," Odus said.

"It's either him or me," Katy said.

Odus glanced at Sue and then nodded. "Fine. Let's roll."

CHAPTER TWENTY-SEVEN

Sarah didn't know what to make of this little get-together.

She'd locked the front door, but didn't rightly know whether she was more afraid of whatever was outside or the people inside and of what they might tell her. Odus had made the invites, so he had pretty much staked a claim to being the leader of the bunch. Gordon Smith's widow stood with her teen daughter by the counter, biting at her lip like she wished she could be anywhere else. The Chesterfield clock above the door showed a quarter 'til ten, nearly her bedtime, but she had a feeling she wouldn't be sleeping tonight.

She brought a full coffee pot to the table as Odus laid a fire in the woodstove. The general store's floor was without insulation, and the weather had turned colder with sunset, an arctic air mass making an early entry from the Northwest. The assembled lot was about as ill-fitting as the wintry wind outside.

Claude Tester slouched on a bench. The Rev. Mose Eldreth sat erect, his elbows on the table as if he were about to pray. Kim Deister dealt cheese crackers from a cellophane pack and crunched them, the only sound in the room besides the crackling fire. Kim's right hand was swathed in gauze and tape. Sue Norwood stood to one side, playing with a wind chime, not far from where the mouse-munching goat had passed not more than four hours ago. The Smith widow, Katy, was off in the corner with the pickled eggs and chewing tobacco like she'd rather be anywhere else, but her plucky daughter with the shoe-black hair and makeup seemed all too eager for adventure.

Kim's blonde hair featured pink highlights, and Jett's bore a blue streak. Sarah never thought she'd live long enough to see such a thing in Solom, but she'd passed way too many years already, and it was starting to catch up with her. Starting in her arthritic joints and working up to her addled brain.

"Come have a seat, Miss Norwood," Sarah said. "Got some drip grind right here."

"Half off?" Odus asked with a crooked grin. He seemed to be in a better mood tonight, or maybe he'd just hit the Old Crow enough to smooth off his rough edges.

"I'll take half off your head if you keep talking like this. We're supposed to be serious."

"Hard to be serious when the Horseback Preacher is back in the saddle."

Sue sat beside Mose, in one of the wooden-slatted chairs with uneven legs. The preacher nodded to her. Sarah sat a Styrofoam cup in front of her and filled it before Sue could say whether or not she wanted some.

When all the cups were full, she put the coffee pot on top of the woodstove and sat at the table with the others. Odus tossed a splintery chunk of locust into the stove and closed the cast-iron mouth, then stood and looked around the dining area.

"I reckon we all know each other," Odus said. "So let's just get right to it. The plain truth of it is Harmon's come back to Solom and all hell's about to break loose."

Claude shook his head. "You've been in the bourbon. Only a drunk would talk like that."

"He's here."

"Harmon Smith is dead and planted, long gone to dust. That's just an old wives' tale."

"Speaking of wives, then, where's yours?"

Claude shut up at that, but Sue cut in with, "Can you tell us more about Harmon Smith? Not all of us here were weaned on the legends."

"The Horseback Preacher," Mose said in his own preaching voice. "Some call him the Man in the Black Hat or the Circuit Rider. He rode these mountains in the early 1800s as a Methodist, set him up a homestead and a garden. He was a little touched in the head, though, and started bucking the Methodist beliefs, turned to sacrificing animals in the Old Testament fashion. They say he was murdered on a mountain trail one night. Some believe it was fellow Methodists who did him in; others say it was the Solom folks who had begun to follow his ways."

"I reckon they figured if animal sacrifice made God happy, then offering up a human ought to do wonders," Odus said. "But he didn't stay dead."

"Sounds like so much horse shit to me," Claude said.

"There are ladies present," David said.

Claude nodded angrily at Kim. "What's she doing here anyway?"

"She's an Army vet. Figured we could use some marksmanship."

"Fort Meade, among other places," Kim said, with no false pride but with no backdown either. "I was a specialist in Linguistics and Cryptology.

"That's just dandy if they taught you to speak goat, or hold one of them séance things and talk to them beyond the grave," Claude said.

"Women held Solom together through the Civil War, the two world wars, and lots of shenanigans since then," Sarah said. "I think we can handle a battle."

She ought to jump in and confess that she'd seen the

Horseback Preacher. She'd heard the local legends all her life but managed to ignore them. Jews had their dybbuks and golems, but nowhere did men of God ever come back from the dead to bring suffering to the living.

But *had* the Horseback Preacher brought suffering? In all the stories she'd heard, the man did nothing more than appear, like the Virgin Mary on a grilled cheese sandwich, or the devil in the clouds of those mocked-up photos that graced the cover of the "Weekly World News." Sure, some claimed he caused calamity and death, but plain bad luck could account for a lot of the mishaps. Maybe he was more like an escort, the effect rather than the cause.

What did the man say to her? *I'm back.* Like it was neither a brag nor a threat, just a plain fact, something he held no power or choice over.

"It's one of those things where you need to make believers out of people," Odus said. "No offense, Elder Mose, but your branch of Baptists don't go in for conversion."

Sue raised her hand, like the new student in a grade school class. "Sorry, folks, but I don't get any of this, and I'm still not sure what we're supposed to do about it."

Katy spoke for the first time. "Doesn't matter. We didn't ask for him to pay a visit to the Smith farm, but he showed up anyway. I have a hard time believing he's evil. He saved our lives."

"So the rumors are true?" Mose asked. "About what happened that night?"

"Gordon Smith went crazy and tried to kill us. But he—the Horseback Preacher—sacrificed Gordon instead. He didn't seem like a ghost—he was as solid as this counter." Katy rapped on its surface for effect.

"But nobody's been killed lately," Claude said. "You can't have a good spook story unless there's some blood in it somewhere."

Odus nodded, went around the middle aisle to the dry goods section, and returned stooped over, rolling a battered ten-speed. The wheels wobbled, the chain dragged the floor, and the seat cushion was gouged and pocked. It looked as if it had been trampled by a herd of elephants. "Recognize this?"

"That's one the Everharts rented." Sue said.

"Found it on Switchback Trail, off in the laurels. No sign of the couple, just a bunch of scuffed leaves by the creek. But there was *this*." Odus held up a small flashlight that appeared to have dried blood on the handle.

"I told you we should have called the cops," Sue said.

"What for?" Odus said. "This is Solom's problem. It's our job to take care of it. Besides, what would we tell them? That a man a hundred and fifty years dead has come back to square things with them that did him in?"

"Hold on," Kim said. "You don't really think this is supernatural, do you?"

"I just know what I seen. What about you, Elder Mose?"

Mose lowered his eyes. The stove popped in the gap of silence, and the long stovepipe ticked with rising heat. Hickory smoke that escaped during the igniting of the fire now settled in a blue-gray layer five feet off the floor. Sarah wished for a chore, another pot of coffee or a round of sandwiches to give out on the house.

"Sarah?" Odus challenged her, his blue eyes piercing hers, somehow harder to meet since they weren't bloodshot. "You saw him, didn't you?"

Sarah looked at the counter and the glass mayonnaise jar by the register with the change in it. The jar held donations for Rupert Walpole, a retired postal carrier who developed cancer of the larynx. As if a few dollars could make any difference once the cancer dug its claws into you. Just like the Horseback

Preacher wormed his way into Solom's heart as a chronic cancer.

"He came in, all right," she said. "Walked right up to the cash register like he was born here and knew every inch of this community. How can that be, if he's been dead all this time?"

Claude gave a rat-squeak of laughter. "Tell us, Brother Mose. I bet you got it all figured out, with your Bible and your big words. You're the one who's big on believing things you can't see."

"I believe in the Lord," Mose said. "But the Good Book allows for the mysterious and miraculous."

Kim stood up. "I'm sorry, Mose. This is getting too wacky for me. I need to get home."

"And do what, Kim?" Mose said. "Tend to your goats?" He nodded at her wounded hand. "*Feed* them?"

Kim sat.

"I guess that brings us to the goats," Sarah said.

"I saw one," Sue said. "Down by the river. It must have got out of its fence."

"One of them bit Kim, then chased her into the house," Mose said. "It would be funny if it wasn't so gosh-darned creepy."

"They been breeding like rabbits this year," Odus said, letting the bike rest against a chain-saw sculpture. "Seems like everybody's got a herd, and they're acting more ornery than usual."

"What about you, Katy Logan?" Sarah said. "You've got the one of the biggest herds on this side of the county. If anything funny's going on with the animals, you'd probably know about it."

"They're...normal," Jett said. "Just goats."

"I heard Betsy Ward had a fainting spell and is in the

hospital, but I've been too busy to call on her," Katy said. "Now I'm starting to wonder. Arvel's been acting jumpy lately."

"Remember the last time the goats got uppity?" Claude said.

"Yeah," Odus said. "Right before Gordon's first wife got killed in that car wreck."

"Shit fire and fart brimstone," Claude said. "If the Horseback Rider is hooked up with the goats somehow...sounds like hell's worst nightmare."

"No matter what they say about Harmon Smith, he was a man of God," Mose said. "I just can't believe God would send anything to His Earth unless there was a good reason."

"God don't need no devil, does He?" Claude taunted. "He's done decided who's going to heaven, so what's the point? Ain't that what you're preaching to the flock, Brother?"

"You ought to come to a service once in a while," Mose said. "Might do you good to get down on your knees and wash somebody's feet."

"Save the feud for later and let's worry about the Horseback Preacher," Odus said. "I ain't ever been sure whether Jesus Christ is going to return or not, but I know for a fact that Harmon Smith has."

"Do you think he—or it, whatever *it* is—killed the Everharts?" Sue asked.

"I don't know." Odus stroked his beard, picked something from the hairs and stared at it. "If he took them, he might be done. But why would he kill two this time?"

Kim took her coffee cup away from her lips. The white rim was ragged, and the perfect imprint of her teeth showed where she'd been biting into the Styrofoam. "Well, even if we accept what you're saying, and we've got a vengeful preacher in our midst, what in the world are we supposed to do about it?"

"That's what this meeting's about," Odus said. "Any ideas?" He looked around the room.

Sarah shook her head. She was determined not to get dragged into this mess. Who cared if goats wandered her aisles and a stranger in black stopped by once in a while? As long as her routine didn't change, and the Horseback Preacher didn't do away with her best customers, she was willing to live and let live.

If such a thing applied to dead people.

"I guess this isn't a garlic-and-crucifix kind of thing, is it?" Sue asked. "I mean, nobody's come up with a mythology. I'd almost rather tackle a vampire or werewolf, something that followed rules."

"You're the Bible guy," Odus said to Mose. "What do you make of it?"

"Harmon Smith seemed to follow some of the Celtic ideas of harvest sacrifice," Mose said. "Gordon Smith was apparently acting out some of those same beliefs, only elevated to a sick fetish."

"He was sick, all right," Katy said. "Coming at us with that scythe, claiming he wanted to please Harmon Smith with a blood sacrifice."

"Every religious figure needs a flock," Kim said. "Without Moonies, Sun Myung Moon would have been just another businessman."

"Moon do what?" Ray said.

"The leader of the Unification Church," she said. "He established a church in Washington, D.C., and owned a ton of real estate and international newspapers. The conspiracy theorists believed Moon's mouth was whispering in the ear of our politicians while his fingers were slipping cash into their back pockets. Some say even the president was an ally."

"Now don't you be knocking the president," Claude said. "The worst thing that ever happened to Solom was letting Republicans come in. If Bush was a Jew, he'd have been the Antichrist."

Sarah didn't rise to the bait, though she made a mental note of his remark. Her father changed the family name from Jaffe to Jeffers before moving to Solom. She'd never made a big deal about being Jewish, though she was the only one in the valley. She wasn't all that religious, anyway, and she sold plenty of knick-knacks that featured Bible verses or pictures of a snow-white Christ.

"Maybe the goats tie in with fertility and harvest," Mose said. "The more you sacrifice, the more they multiply. The Old Testament sacrifices were all about appeasing a wrathful God. It's the same with most religions, whether you're lighting candles, taking communion, shaving your head, or offering food."

"All I know is the billy goats don't like it when you talk about gelding them," Kim said, holding up her injured hand.

"Can't blame them," Jett said. "I don't even have balls, and that makes *me* wince."

"Hold on a minute, folks," Sue said. "I can accept that the Horseback Preacher is real. After all, every legend has a basis in fact. And I'll even buy that goats are evil. I mean, with those creepy eyes and cloven hooves, how could anybody think otherwise? And let's assume 'its hour come round,' as the Yeats poem goes, and Solom is our backwoods Bethlehem of the Damned. After all, the battle of Armageddon has to start somewhere. Now what?"

They all looked at each other, except Kim, who was staring into the bottom of her coffee cup as if the answer was spelled out there. "I reckon we have to find a way to take down the Horseback Preacher," Odus said. "We have to figure out what he wants, then give it to him and make him go away."

"What if he won't go until he takes us all with him?" Claude said.

Sarah suddenly felt all alone, even in the presence of company. She imagined the general store under the great crushing weight of night. Despite the ticking wood stove, a chill settled into her brittle bones. Darkness pressed against the window, and the porch light did little to scare it off.

Black was every color rolled into one, they said, and when everything bled together it made just the one color, the absence of light. And it looked like there was going to be plenty of bleeding going on.

A clatter arose from the front of the store, near the register. She'd turned off the lights as she usually did at closing time, and the corners of the store were cloaked in shadows.

"Who's there?' she said. Nobody could have broken in without her hearing. But somehow that mouse-eating goat passed through these walls, and a man who could command goats and defy the grave probably wouldn't be considerate enough to knock. Besides. he'd already paid her a visit once.

The Horseback Preacher stepped into the light. He held a pack of Beechnut chewing tobacco in his hand, and as they watched, he slowly peeled the foil pack open and shoved a moist wad into his mouth, shreds of the dark tobacco dribbling down his chin to the floor. The brim of his hat was turned low, but the bottom half of his face was waxen and milk-colored, not as ghostly as when Sarah had first seen him. His mouth was filled with broad, blunt teeth, like those of a grazing animal.

"Put it on my tab, Sarah," he said, grinding the tobacco with his jaws, his voice cob-rough and deep.

"What business you got here in Solom?" said Odus, the first of them to recover.

"No business, just pleasure," he said.

A whinny came from outside, near the front of the store. The Horseback Preacher plucked a Macintosh apple out of a bushel basket. He polished it against the sleeve of his black wool jacket. "Know them by their fruits."

Kim spilled her coffee and Odus backed up until he bumped into the woodstove. Mose raised half out of his chair and stood there, bent over as if he'd been flash frozen. Sarah thought about the shotgun under the cash register, but it was still covered by newspapers.

"Nice of you folks to hold this little get-together for my sake," he said. "I'm touched."

"We don't want nothing from you," Odus said. "We just want to be left alone. We're willing to let you rest in peace."

"Love your enemies, right, Elder Mose? The New Testament says to turn the other cheek but the Old Testament says an eye for an eye. I go in for tradition, myself."

The Horseback Preacher gave a laugh that held no humor, with just the hint of a hellwind behind it. He shot a thick stream of tobacco onto the pine floor boards, causing Sarah to wince. Touching the brim of his hat, he dipped his head slightly, as if nodding to the ladies.

"Sorry to rush off, but I have work waiting in the orchards of life," he said. He went to the door, his boots loud on the wood, then opened it and went outside, merging into the darkness from which he'd come. From which they all had come, and to which they were inevitably bound.

Hooves thundered down the asphalt road, and the eight people waited in silence, afraid to give words to their fear. Eventually, Sarah went to get a rag and mop up the tobacco stain. By the time she reached the spot by the register, the dark stain had vanished, as elusive as the creature that had left its mark.

CHAPTER TWENTY-EIGHT

The sun came up on a brisk, clear Sunday.

Frost laid a sparkling skin across the ground, but quickly melted where touched by the autumn light. Odus had slept uneasily, visions of the Horseback Preacher galloping across his eyes whenever he happened to drift.

He tried to remember what Granny Hampton said about the Horseback Preacher, if the old-timers commanded some means of warding him off. Didn't seem likely, because even after all these years, Solom was still a stopping point for Harmon Smith.

The other mountain communities on Harmon's original rounds had probably all seen their share of mishap and death. Odus would bet that anybody following the histories of Balsam, Parson's Ford, Windshake, Rocky Knob, and Crowder Valley would see a trail marked by bloody hoof prints. The Horseback Preacher covered a lot of territory, stretching into East Tennessee and Virginia, and even a man on a hell-driven horse could only cover so many miles in a day.

Odus dressed in a pair of overalls that were dirty and stiff, but he'd aired out for a couple of days until they were bearable. He scrambled a couple of eggs and rummaged in the counter. Like any common drunk, he knew exactly how much liquor was in the house. On a Sunday, a bottle would be hard to come by unless he felt like visiting a bootlegger and paying a king's ransom.

Odus had tucked back a pint of Old Crow, and the bourbon lay golden and gleaming in the glass, greasy and somehow thicker than water. He'd been tempted to polish it off last night, especially after Harmon walked into the general store pretty as a show pony, as if knowing they were talking about him and daring them to make a play.

But liquor tasted better on a Sunday and mock courage might serve where plain old backbone failed.

Because Odus was going to hunt down the Horseback Preacher.

After Harmon mounted Old Saint and vanished into the dark, off toward whatever errands called such a creature, Odus and the group had gone onto the general store's porch. The others were shaken, excepting old Sarah, who'd been around for a few of Harmon's past visits, though she claimed this was the first time she'd ever seen him up close. Sure, Mose Eldreth talked big, quoting some Bible passages from books that Odus had never heard before, with names like Nehemiah and Malachi, but he was as scared as the rest.

Mose quoted Malachi as having set down these words in the old days, back when pretty near everybody with a beard, a high fever, and a clay tablet could be a prophet: "Surely the day is coming, it will burn like a furnace. All the arrogant and every evildoer will be stubble. The fruit will wither on the vine."

Then Mose went on to say that the dead horseback preacher had been quoting from the Book of Matthew, when Christ delivered his Sermon on the Mount.

Odus didn't feel much like an evildoer. Sure, he cheated the government and big corporations and rich Floridian tourists, but he never cheated a human being. His reputation as a handyman was built on his word. He delivered what he promised, and he was never a day late about it, either. He treated people fair and expected the same.

That was more than Odus could rightly say of the Lord, at

least from what he'd witnessed in his time on this Earth. So he couldn't see why the Lord would want to set something like the Horseback Preacher loose on Solom, especially since most of them were decent, church-going folks.

But it didn't matter whether Harmon had ridden up through the gates of hell or whether he'd clopped down a set of golden stairs. Odus could track the Horseback Preacher because, ghostly stallion or not, the animal left hoof prints in the muddy parking lot.

With a flashlight, Odus followed the tracks until they disappeared on the asphalt of Railroad Grade Road, although the prints faded and vanished within minutes of its passing. Chances were that Harmon was hiding out up in the woods, probably on his original land at the foot of Lost Ridge where the Smith House sat. Even a dead man probably took comfort in familiar surroundings.

Odus hadn't mentioned his plan to the others because he didn't see that they could offer any help. Claude had a country lick of sense, but he was too steamed at Preacher Mose to work as a group. Sarah had too many years on her, Sue Norwood was too young, Kim was too sensible, and Mose couldn't shake free of his Bible enough to tackle such a thing.

Katy and Jett...well, he liked them and felt a need to protect them. This was Solom's troubles, and they had suffered enough.

Odus hunted in the fall, and usually got himself two or three bucks each season. The venison could be frozen or canned, and he traded the meat for vegetables and fruit. It was another way to keep from holding down a regular job. Now the tracking skills would come in handy, although a Winchester 30-30 wouldn't do the same job on Harmon Smith that it did on a white-tailed deer.

Odus figured he'd find the right weapon when the time

came. If Mose could afford faith, then so could Odus.

He threw a can of Vienna sausages, a couple of McIntosh apples, a thermos of coffee, and the bottle of Old Crow in his leather hunting pouch, hauled it and his fishing rod to the truck, and headed for the river road.

CHAPTER TWENTY-NINE

Alex fired up a bowl of sweet, home-grown weed and puffed it until his lungs were scorched.

Despite the pleasant buzz from the smoke, Alex couldn't relax. Something heavy was coming down in Solom. He had a feeling it wasn't the secret agents he'd always feared, or the Internal Revenue Service coming to seize his land as punishment for his tax evasion. No, this exhibited all the vibes of a global conspiracy.

Alex had convinced Meredith to stay in her apartment near the college. Despite her sweet charms and generosity, Alex liked his space. He needed to get his head together, which seemed to be a full-time job these days. He put the pipe away and went outside to check on the garden.

The garden did what drugs and sex couldn't do: it filled him with a sense of purpose and accomplishment. Growing good crops, especially mythical motherlode mindfuck marijuana, was about as close to God as a human being could get. Crops made the world a better place, especially dope, which was the equivalent of Eden's apple when it came to granting wisdom.

As a fringe benefit, self-reliance also stuck it to the Man, because the government hadn't yet figured out how to tax it. He'd considered moving to one of the legal-marijuana states, but he wasn't willing to become part of the Establishment in order to sell weed. Seemed like the worst kind of compromise.

Alex peeked through the curtains to make sure nobody was watching from outside. Dope possessed the strange power to make him feel bulletproof and paranoid at the same time. Behind the safety of locked doors, he was master of his fate. When he stepped under the big sky, all manner of rules and laws took effect, whether they were natural or contrived by the global elite to ensure that nothing changed, that all the stars stayed fixed in the heavens and all the crooks in Congress defended their incumbency.

Looked safe outside. No cops, no Weird Dude Walking. The morning sun poured its pink-orange lava over the eastern ridges and the woods were on fire with autumn. It was nearly ten o'clock, which meant the bell in the steeple of the Free Will Baptist Church would soon sound its Sunday call. Birds twittered in the surrounding trees, as sacred a music as any that ever droned from a church organ. If the birds were talking, that meant everything was normal, despite the eerie flutter in the pit of his stomach.

Alex went out onto the deck, binoculars in hand. Through a cut where the road wound among the trees, the Smith farm was visible. Focusing the lenses, he saw the Smith widow, the redhead, walking toward the barn. Alex didn't like spying, because it was too close to what the CIA practiced against its own citizens. But survival instinct told him there was a big difference between being nosy and being informed.

As he watched, the redhead veered toward the fence, then pulled back as a clutch of goats came trotting toward her from the rear of the barn. Probably the same damn goats that had eaten Weird Dude Walking.

Alex shortened the lenses so he could scan his fence line. The spot he'd repaired near the garden was still intact. He'd fantasized about planting some sort of booby trap, maybe a razor-studded spring that could be triggered by a trip wire. But the fence was technically on Smith property, and that would be crossing the line. Trespassing was uncool, even if their livestock fed on old preachers as if they were a Jesus biscuit in a Catholic chow line.

Alex put down the binoculars. All was right with the world, at least his portion of it.

Then he saw the shed.

The doors were open, one of them hanging askew on a single hinge. The grow bulbs threw their blue-tinted light against the greater might of the orange sun. Something had forcibly broken in, or maybe *out*. There was nothing in the shed of value except...

Thirty-seven of Mother Nature's most beautiful creatures.

His babies. His family.

Alex hurtled down the deck steps three at a time, the binoculars swinging from the strap and banging against his chest. He ran the fifty feet to the shed and looked in, barely able to breathe.

Most of the pot plants had been ripped up by the roots, though a few bare and broken stalks poked toward the ceiling like skeletal green fingers. Stray leaves lay scattered along the floor, and one light fixture dangled by wires from the wall. The black plastic sheeting beneath the buckets was ripped and gouged. And on the cinder blocks that served as a step was a mucosal gray-white smear that could only be one thing.

Goat shit.

The fuckers trespassed onto *his* land, broken into *his* shed, chomped down on the fruit of *his* labors. He didn't know how they'd circumvented the fence or busted through the doors, but the ground was scarred by cloven-hoofed footprints. Alex, his heart pushing broken glass through his chest, followed the tracks behind the shed to the fence.

There, the wire was trampled as if pressed down by a great weight, dragging down several locust posts. The wire was pocked with tufts of goat hair, and the musky stench of a rutting billy tainted the air.

On the Smith side of the fence, leaves had been scuffed and scooted around. Clearly evident against the dark humus was the imprint of a horseshoe. As if some rider urged his horse to stomp down the fence and allow the goats access. Maybe the horse kicked in the shed door for them. Alex was sure that, if he checked beside the padlock, he'd find the arc of a horseshoe embedded in the wood.

Alex wondered if Weird Dude Walking was no longer walking. Maybe he'd mounted up in order to make better time. On whatever road he was headed down.

Didn't matter.

The Dude had fucked with private property. And so had those creepy-eyed, stink-making, beard-pissing goats.

The Bible said to forgive trespasses, but Alex didn't hold to the Bible. In Alex's belief system, trespasses meant one of two things: either you build a bigger fence or you go after those who didn't respect boundaries.

Alex went back to the house, to the walk-in closet that held his arsenal. There was hell to pay and Alex planned on delivering the invoice.

CHAPTER THIRTY

"Jett?" Katy called from the yard. "Hey, Jett."

Like most teens, Jett liked to sleep as late as she could, especially on Sundays, but after the meeting at the general store, both of them endured restless nights. Katy usually asked Jett do farm chores on weekends, but this morning she was glad to be out of the claustrophobia of the house. She'd been a little groggy but her discovery at the barn yanked her fully alert.

Jett, still in her pajamas, came out on the porch rubbing her eyes. "You don't have to yell loud enough to wake the dead. I'm here already."

"Did you leave the gate open?"

"No, we put up the goats before we went to the general store."

"Somebody let them out, then."

"Maybe they pushed the gate open," Jett said. "You know how they love to butt everything in the world and rub against the fence. Besides, they're all in the pen, right?"

Katy gave the herd the once-over. They were so agitated she couldn't do a full count, but there were no noticeable absences. "Looks like it."

"What's the big deal, then?"

"Just a little jumpy, I guess. You go on and get dressed and I'll be in to make us some pancakes in a minute."

"Don't step in anything." Jett went back in the house.

Katy waded through the herd to the feed bins. Usually the goats followed but this morning they stood where they were, watching her pass. Dirty Harry shook his head from side to side, causing his matted beard to sway. She was almost relieved to reach the barn's interior. She opened the bin and banged open the metal trash can that held the grain. The chickens gathered around as she dumped a few scoops on the barn floor.

Even though the pastures still held a little forage, the goats enjoyed their morning hay. Katy climbed the loft stairs for hay, and when she swung open the heavy wooden door, there was too much open space.

Then she realized scarecrows were missing.

Would Jett play that kind of joke on me?

No, unless Jett had snuck out in the middle of the night, she wouldn't have had an opportunity. Besides, Jett was more afraid of the scarecrows than she was the goats, even though the effigies were nothing more than cloth and straw.

She grabbed a pitchfork, more for comfort than defense, and backed her way downstairs to the barn door. The goats gathered behind her, their curiosity aroused. Horns bumped her bottom and she spun, nearly jabbing the rusty tines into Dirty Harry's face.

"Make way or die," she said.

The goats closed in, sealing off her exit.

This can't be happening.

But she had already endured the impossible here in Solom.

The goats peeled back their lips and bleated, showing their stained teeth. What looked like dark rags hung from some of the mouths. Had the goats somehow reached the scarecrows?

She plucked a fragment from between a mottled nanny's teeth. It snapped at her fingers as she drew the scrap of cloth away. The fabric dripped clotted red fluid. She sniffed it.

Blood?

The nanny leaped into the air and clacked its teeth

together, snatching for the treat. Katy dropped it and wiped her hand on the thigh of her jeans. Dirty Harry pressed his nose against the stain and sniffed.

She swatted at him with the handle of the pitchfork, delivering a *thwack* across his flank. His nostrils flared and his vertical pupils took on an odd light. The goats surrounded her, blocking her escape to the house. She flung the pitchfork at the gathering tribe and fled toward the barn stairs. She could have reached one of the holding pens first, but then she'd be trapped. In the loft, she'd have options.

Even as she thundered up the uneven wooden steps, she realized how ridiculous her plight was. All her resolve to disconnect these animals from Gordon Smith's attack and the Horseback Preacher's appearance withered away with one hungry look. Now they were nightmares on the hoof.

But even worse things could be waiting in the loft.

Such as Gordon, back from the grave and wearing the scarecrow costume? Or the real Scarecrow Man, climbing down from his wire to finish what Gordon started?

But the loft held only hay and dust, the morning sunlight sending great golden shafts across the buckling plank floor. She secured the door behind her as goat hooves pounded on the steps.

The far end of the loft featured a sliding door. Odus and Ray Tester had backed a truckload of bales up to the door and hauled them up a wooden ladder to the loft. The ladder must be there among the yellow bales stacked along both sides of the loft. If not, she'd have to kick the mesh wiring out of a window and jump twenty-five feet to the ground.

The ladder was there, half buried in spilled piles of straw. She unlatched the heavy door and slid it open, the metal track from which it hung squealing with the weight.

"Mom?" Jett said from the yard below. "What's going

on?"

"I told you to stay in the house."

"I heard you scream. What did you expect me to do?"

"I didn't scream."

"Yes, you did. Now quit freaking out."

"That wasn't a scream, it was…a shout of dismay."

"Whatever."

"Watch out for the goats, they—"

"I shut the barn door so they couldn't get out. I could tell they were acting weird again."

"Okay, good. Help me with this ladder so I don't break my leg."

She wrestled the ladder over to the opening and slid it over the lip of the floor until Jett could reach the bottom. Once it was securely planted in the ground, Katy swung onto it and clambered down.

Something thumped against the barn walls.

"Head butt," Jett said.

More thumping. The siding planks quivered.

"Damn, they're going to bust through." Katy grabbed Jett's hand and pulled her toward the house.

"No way, Mom. They're just goats."

"You heard the people at the general store last night. The goats are part of whatever's happening in Solom."

"So we just board ourselves in like it's 'Night of the Living Zombie Goat'?"

"For starters." Katy reached the gate first and waited for Jett, and then swung it closed. The inside of the barn was a clattering cacophony of horns and hooves battering the walls. The tin roof gave off a metallic echo as if the valley were filled with thunder. A plank broke free from the side of the barn and a gleaming eye appeared in the gap.

Jett sprinted for the porch as another plank broke loose.

Katy was right behind her, and she slammed and locked the door when they were both inside. They went to the living room window and parted the curtains just enough to watch. Dirty Harry was halfway out the gap in the siding, his front forelegs suspended in the air and kicking wildly. He thrashed his head from side to side, wallowing the planks loose around him.

Soon he squirted free as another board splintered and cracked, then two more goats followed the filthy billy. They kicked through and then the rest of the tribe poured forth and milled restlessly in the pen. Dirty Harry reared up and planted his feet on the wire fence, pushing it to the ground.

"Man, talk about a jailbreak," Jett said.

As soon as the fence was stomped to the ground, the goats stampeded, heading down the driveway.

"At least they're not headed for the house," Katy said.

"Do we call Odus to round them up?"

"Just between me and you, I think they've earned their freedom."

"So you're saying you're chicken?"

"I'm making a conservative decision."

Jett shook her head as the goats trotted past the cornfield and headed for the Ward farm. "I hope our insurance covers this."

"Come on," Katy said. "Let's make those pancakes."

"Shouldn't we warn people?"

"It's just a bunch of goats. They can take care of themselves."

"That's what I'm afraid of."

CHAPTER THIRTY-ONE

The Horseback Preacher somehow found his faithful horse and was mobile again, but Odus was eager to track him.

Odus figured he would either be at one of his three Lost Ridge grave sites or else up on the Snakeberry Trail where he'd been killed. He'd need a horse himself if he was going to roam the back-mountain trails. A motorcycle would probably work better, but the engine noise would kill any element of surprise. Plus he didn't think he could hotwire a Harley without rousing half the police in the county.

Besides, it seemed only proper to track the Horseback Preacher by horseback. Since Odus was going into this showdown without any weapons, he figured he ought to make up the rules as he went along, on the theory that like could slay like.

Odus parked his truck on a gravel lot by the river at the McHenry farm. He was near the bridge that led to Rush Branch Road, a steep strip of crumbled asphalt that gave way to mud as it wound around the mountain. The Smith property lay on the other side, in the valley at the base of the mountain.

The Primitive Baptist Church stood near the peak, just where the pavement ended. Some three-story houses were perched on the steep slopes here and there, up where the late wind shook the walls, but they were mostly summer homes for Yankees and were empty this time of year. It would be easy to ignore their fences and "No Trespassing" signs. The Horseback Preacher certainly wouldn't observe human laws, and Odus better adopt that same mindset.

He found a horse on a riverside pasture, a stretch of flat bottom land that would have been developed for condos already if not for the spring floods that sometimes washed over it. The horse was a pinto mare of mixed colors, probably two or three years old. It shied away as Odus approached, which was just fine because Odus needed to lure the horse out of sight of the river road.

The horse was pastured with cows, a mistake on Old Man McHenry's part, because horses didn't know how to behave after spending time with cud-chomping sacks of sirloin. Odus helped McHenry put up some hay last fall and knew his way around the barn. The house was up the road a quarter mile, so Odus was concealed while he rummaged. The horse followed him to the barn because it smelled the apple in Odus's pocket and, despite the bad bovine influence, an apple to a horse was like a sweet lie to a woman. They both got you what you wanted.

In the barn, Odus rounded up a halter and reins. He didn't like sliding the steel bit in the horse's mouth. Folks said horses didn't mind, but it looked uncomfortable anyway. He gave the pinto the apple to work on while he cinched the saddle. Odus had ridden here and there in his work as a hired hand, occasionally putting in some saddle time to exercise horses for lazy people. He was no John Wayne, or even Gene Autry, but he knew enough to keep from getting bucked.

The church crowd would be filling the roads any minute now, and he'd have to either use the bridge or find a shallow spot to cross Blackburn River. He liked the idea of fording the river. That's probably how the Horseback Preacher did it. With any luck, or some kind of higher power pitching in a little help, Odus would be able to track Harmon before nightfall.

Because night was a time when things like dead preachers

grew more powerful. Odus didn't need a scientist to tell him that. Dark things loved the dark, and the dark loved them right back.

Odus swung in the saddle and gave the pinto a twitch on her flank. "You got a name?" he asked her.

The horse whinnied, spraying a few specks of apple.

"I'll take that as a 'Yep,'" Odus said. "You speak human better than I speak horse so I'll just have to make something up. Harmon has Old Saint, so let's call you 'Sister Mary.' What do you think of that?"

Sister Mary's snort might have signaled disgust, or it could have been a request for another apple. Either way, she headed out of the barn when he gave the reins a shake. He guided Sister Mary past the cows, who stared as if they'd bought tickets, and toward the river.

Just before Sister Mary put a tentative hoof in the cold water, Odus glanced up the ridge at the next pasture. McHenry's goats were lined along the fence, watching them, as menacing as the Apache warriors in a wagon train western.

"Don't pay them no mind," Odus said. "We got business elsewhere."

He gently bounced his knees against Sister Mary's ribs and they entered the current.

CHAPTER THIRTY-TWO

He only takes one.

That had been the way of Solom for as far back as the legends reached. All a body needed to do was keep his head down, stay inside, and wait for somebody else to get claimed. That philosophy served Arvel well for sixty-eight years and counting. As a boy, when he'd first seen the Horseback Preacher on the little pig path that led to his Rush Branch fishing hole, he'd managed to escape for some reason.

He'd tried to tell his dad, a no-nonsense, up-with-the-sun Free Will Baptist, about the encounter, but Dad cut him off at the first mention. The Horseback Preacher wasn't real, and that was that, and no amount of blabbing and blubbering would change that. Except Dad's wrinkled-raisin face had grown as pale as a potato root, leaving Arvel to wonder if Dad might have undergone his own little run-in with the dead preacher.

Arvel kept himself scarce for the next two days, feigning a bellyache so he wouldn't have to go to school or do chores. That wasn't much of a stretch, because he was so nervous he puked every time a spoonful of food hit his gut. From the bedroom he shared with his brother Zeke, he could see the Smith barn, and under the moonlight shadows sometimes moved in the hayloft. He'd clamp his eyes tight, but one of them would end up creeping open like the lid of a vampire's coffin. He didn't sleep much those two days.

Then, his brother didn't come home from school. The county schools ran buses, and the Wards and other kids in their area walked a mile down to the river to catch one. The bus stop was a favorite spot for shenanigans, with a dozen kids of different ages killing time with jokes, cutting on the signpost with pocket knives, and the occasional round of post office or show-me-yours-and-I'll-show-you-mine.

Zeke had taken up cigarettes, another time killer, but none of the other kids dared smoke. Of course, that made Zeke the idol of the dirt-road neighborhood, but he also knew he would get his rear end worn to a pile of rags if the folks caught him. The kids say he showed them the pack of cigarettes that morning, unfiltered Viceroys in a shiny pack he must have swiped from the general store.

As big a show-off as he was, Zeke thought he'd best slip off into the woods to do his puffing. Arvel guessed his brother was just as afraid of coughing and hacking in front of the others as he was of being spied by an adult. Whatever the reason, Zeke went into a laurel scrub and lit up.

The kids watched for the trail of smoke to be sure that Zeke wasn't joshing them, then turned their attention back to their games. It was only when the bus rolled up and one of the kids hollered Zeke's name that they realized he'd been gone way too long to just smoke a cigarette.

Arvel's best friend, J.C. Littlejohn, went into the laurel to find Zeke. The bus driver honked and the other kids shouted names, according to J.C., but Zeke didn't come out of hiding. J.C. found him sprawled on the ground, belly down, the moist butt of the Viceroy inches from his lips, the ember on the lit end burning a hole in a dead leaf. Zeke's Ked sneaker had lodged in a protruding root and he'd tripped.

Freak accident, the county coroner said. His forehead hit a tree trunk and snapped his neck back, killing him instantly.

And Arvel's first thought upon hearing the news: *I'm glad the Horseback Preacher took him instead of me.*

He was having a similar thought now. Betsy was home from the hospital and was going to be just fine. That was the trouble. Arvel was hoping Betsy would be the one the Horseback Preacher took this time. Not that he wished ill of Betsy, but after all these years, he was still so sweat-shaky scared of Harmon Smith, he'd rather die a thousand different ways rather than end up done in by him. Because them that the preacher claimed had a way of showing back up.

Arvel saw his brother a decade after his death, when Arvel was newly married and had taken over running the farm after Daddy's final stroke. Arvel made a habit of keeping watch on the Smith barn, and his adolescence was haunted not by his brother's fluke accident, but by the shifting wedges of darkness that seemed to cavort just beyond the sunlit windows.

On a cold March morning, when Arvel was on his way to slop the two hogs, Zeke was standing by the collard patch, barely visible, wreathed in the fog as if he were woven into it. His head lolled to one side like an onion hanging by a piece of twine.

"Soon as he finds his horse, you can come join me," Zeke said, the words seeping out of the mist as if growing up from the dirt. "Gets lonely over here waiting."

Arvel dropped the slop bucket, splashing sour milk, table scraps, eggshells, and apple peels on his jeans. He ran back into the house, where Dad saw the smelly clothing and whooped him for spilling the slop. Dad sent him back out to retrieve the bucket, and Arvel had no choice, you didn't cross Dad on pain of death or worse.

Zeke was gone when he reached the spot by the collards. Arvel didn't look too hard for his dead brother. Instead, he found an excuse to hang around the house or work in the barn for the next several days, only venturing to the garden in broad daylight.

And even through the fear of that encounter, another thought pierced through like sunshine through a church's plate-glass window: *I'm glad it was him and not me.*

Which is the same way he felt when he'd come in the kitchen and seen Betsy sprawled on her back by the stove. The gouge in her side was the mystery. The Horseback Preacher wasn't known to mutilate his victims. Sure, they didn't die pretty, but almost always whole.

Some said that Rebecca Smith had been taken by the Horseback Preacher, but Arvel figured that was just a plain old car wreck on a twisty mountain road. Harmon Smith hadn't been seen in the days leading up to her accident, and it hadn't really fit the pattern of the preacher's rounds. Although considering how Gordon Smith went crazy and attacked his wife, maybe there was a lot more to the story than anybody knew.

But the preacher was back now, that was for sure. The first night that Betsy was confined in a Titusville hospital room, Arvel laid awake until 4 a.m., listening for the sound of hoof beats outside, his heart jumping every time Digger let out a bark. Once he'd gone to the window to check on the Smith barn, but the windows were dark and the moon was buried behind the clouds.

Last night, he'd curled up on a couch in the hospital waiting room, a magazine in his lap as if expecting a diagnosis, and napped just enough to have a nightmare of the Horseback Preacher chasing him down the pig path from the fishing hole.

He didn't feel much safer there than he did now at home.

"Arvel?" Betsy called from the bedroom.

"On the way, honey."

He poured a cup of tea for Betsy and checked the lock on

the back door. He didn't know if locks would keep the dead preacher out. For all he knew, the door had been locked when Betsy experienced her little accident. She had no memory of falling or hitting her head, only a headache she compared to the one she'd suffered the morning after Arvel got her drunk on moonshine and became engaged to her the old-fashioned way.

Betsy was local, half Rominger and half Tester, and she knew about the Horseback Preacher, like everyone else who grew up in these parts. She didn't talk about it, and didn't seem to connect her accident with the preacher's return. So there was still a chance that Betsy was the intended victim.

The preacher could certainly do worse: Betsy was a decent cook and didn't run her mouth too much, she was beholden to men and honored the local traditions. She could can a mean batch of relish or sauerkraut, wasn't above butchering a chicken, and she laid there proper when he crawled on top of her to wallow about once a month when he needed satisfaction. Heck, Harmon Smith could give her to Zeke for all he cared.

Arvel didn't know exactly what the preacher did with them after he got them, but he didn't want to find out. All he knew was if he survived this time, he probably wouldn't live long enough for another turn of the Horseback Preacher's wheel. And that was plenty fine with Arvel.

This was Sunday, the very day Harmon Smith had been killed all those years ago. If ever there was a day for the preacher to carry a grudge, this would be it. And no doubt Zeke would be out tonight, maybe hanging around the garden carrying a hoe or flitting through the apple orchard like a shredded kite.

He added a spoonful of sugar to the tea and carried it up the stairs, glad that he wouldn't be alone tonight.

"How you feeling?" he asked.

Betsy was propped up against the headboard with pillows, a white gauze bandage on her head. "Like death warmed over."

"You'll be up and around in no time."

He turned to go back downstairs and check the doors and windows again. Her voice stopped him.

"You think the preacher is going to take me?" she asked.

"Over my dead body."

She gave a pained smile and sipped her tea. "I bet he came back for the Smith widow."

"I don't wish ill on nobody, but that would be fine with me. If Charlie Smith ends up with the property, he'd probably sell me a chunk. Wouldn't mind some of that sweet bottom pasture."

"But no goats, okay?"

"Not a chance in hell."

CHAPTER THIRTY-THREE

Sister Mary proved to be a rugged animal, despite a lifetime spent in the companionship of cows. Odus guided her up the mountains and traversed the roughest trails he could find, twisted paths that were scarcely wide enough for deer. He half expected the horse would put her nose to the ground like a bloodhound and instinctively know they were on the scent of something bad. Odus figured that two hours had passed, and maybe Old Man McHenry had already noticed somebody had stolen his pinto mare.

At one point, the forest gave way to a granite shelf, with rocks settled into the Appalachian soil like droppings from some ancient giant bird. Odus tied Sister Mary to a stunted balsam and gave her some of the bread from his sandwich. As she smacked her lips around it, Odus eased to the edge and looked down in the valley below.

Solom was sprawled like a faded patchwork quilt of yellow meadows, brown forests, and the small gray squares of houses and barns. The river wound like a loose length of spilled yarn through the bottom land, the water white where it tumbled over rocks. The two-lane road followed the river, except for an intersection near the general store where the covered bridge, post office, and Sue Norwood's shop cluttered up the geometry.

This stony promontory looked like the kind of place where the Horseback Preacher would step out and survey the community. Maybe this was part of his original route, back when he was a Methodist preacher sent down from Virginia.

If so, he might have passed his eyes over the green valley and decided it was just the kind of place to set up shop. A Promised Land, of a sort, one maybe just a little bit remote from the eyes of God, where a fellow could practice whatever kind of rituals he wanted.

Sister Mary let loose with a wet snort.

"All right, don't get your neck hairs in a tangle," Odus said. He went back to the horse, unhitched her, and mounted. His rump was a little sore from the jostling ride, but it wasn't sore enough to complain. He pulled the Old Crow from the knapsack and gargled on a two-finger slug. He was slipping the bottle back into the pack when a twig snapped in the thicket behind him.

"Who's there?" Odus said, and despite all his high-spirited notions about not needing a weapon, he wouldn't have minded a rifle right about then. Not that there were any wild animals left in the mountains big enough to threaten a man or a horse. The occasional bobcat was about as predatory as it got these days.

Whatever was thrashing around in the brush didn't answer. Not that Odus expected a reply. He eased Sister Mary down the path a little, wanting to put some distance between them and the cliff edge. Sister Mary seemed to notice her passenger's unease, because her ears pricked up. Odus gave her a pat on the side of the neck to calm her.

He was twenty feet down the path when the goat emerged from the stand of laurels. Odus almost laughed in relief. Except the goat's head was tilted sideways, the way a man might look at a car he was thinking of buying. Or maybe which steak from the butcher's counter he craved for that night's supper. Sister Mary drew up short without Odus having to pull back on the reins.

"Get on," Odus said to the goat. The goat was nearly a

quarter the size of the horse, fat and white, a string of dirty fur trailing from its belly to the ground. Its eyes were rheumy, the corners full of yellow pus. It stank of piss and the musk of its rutting scent. The horns spread wide, with just the slightest bend to them. Its lower jaw dropped, the worn and stained teeth showing in a corrupt grin. Odus recognized the animal now, from the Smith farm's herd.

What's it doing loose up here?

Odus had walked the Smith fence lines in early August, just before the second cutting of the hay. The wire was in good shape, and locust posts took decades to rot. Goats earned a reputation for breaking boundaries and getting into where they weren't wanted, but it didn't make sense for the goat to climb up into the laurel thicket. Laurel leaves were poisonous, and not much else was green this time of year except balsam and jack pine.

The goat didn't look like it cared for green. The strange, glittering pupils fixed on Odus as if the two were gunfighters squaring off in the Old West.

The goat lowered its head, the scruff of beard pressed against the shaggy chest, showing the serrated grooves of the two brown horns. The animal pawed at the ground with one hoof, like a Spanish bull preparing to charge a red cape. A goat was far more dangerous than most people thought, because its neck was strong and horns hard and sharp. If the horns tore into the horse's abdominal cavity, the goat would likely pull away with intestines entwined like spaghetti around a twirled fork. The laurels on each side were too thick and tangled to allow escape.

Odus peeked over his shoulder to see if a path led down the side of the cliff, and that's when the goat charged. It came in low, at Sister Mary's knees. The horse shrieked and bucked, flailing its front legs in the air. Odus clung to the reins and hunched over the horse's neck, one boot flying out of its stirrup. For a moment he was weightless, and then he crashed back down into the saddle, slamming his testicles against the hard leather.

Sister Mary reared again, this time catching the goat in the forehead with one steel-shod hoof. The goat let out a gurgling bleat and drew back, a gash opening just above its eerie eyes, blood flowing down the snout. The goat retreated a few unsteady steps and wobbled a moment as Sister Mary hopped forward, not giving Odus a chance to regain control.

The goat fell to its knees, lapping at its own blood with a grayish-pink tongue. Sister Mary took a long couple of strides and leaped over the goat, once again lifting Odus out of the saddle, with gravity doing its work and plunging him right back down.

Sister Mary galloped along the path, branches slapping at Odus's hands and face. He glanced back and saw the goat was still lapping at its own leaking fluids. They'd traveled perhaps a hundred yards when Odus press his knees against the mare's flanks and urged her to slow down. At last she came to a stop, panting from the effort. Odus reached into the knapsack and treated himself to a shot of bourbon, his hands shaking. Somehow the encounter with the goat was creepier than the Horseback Preacher's uninvited stop at the general store the night before.

One thing was for sure, the Horseback Preacher appeared to have a few friends on his side. All Odus claimed was a pinto horse, a half-pint of eighty-proof, and a stubborn streak. He guided Sister Mary higher into the forest, where the tributary springs that fed Rush Branch squeezed from cracks in the gray, worn granite. In the world's oldest mountains, where the headwaters of one of the oldest rivers leaked like the tears of a tired widow, Odus figured this was as good a place as any to serve as a cradle of evil.

And Odus planned on rocking that cradle.

CHAPTER THIRTY-FOUR

Sarah usually closed at six in the evening on Sundays, figuring the second shift at the Free Will Baptist Church would bring in a few customers on the way, those who needed a cup of coffee, Moon Pie, or giant Dr. Pepper to fuel them through the service. She couldn't understand why some Baptists felt the need to go to church three or four nights a week. She always thought it would be simpler just to do a little less sinning rather than more begging forgiveness. But a dollar was a dollar, no matter the stains on the soul who spent it.

She'd had only two customers in the past hour, loud Yankee fly fishermen who prowled the aisles and hadn't bought so much as a pack of Wrigley's, although they'd held up a number of the more esoteric items and laughed in that slick, mean way they taught up in New York.

Too many tourists, and Yankees in particular, had a way of waltzing through her store like it was a museum, as if none of the merchandise carried price tags. Like the whole shebang was there for amusement and not to help feed and clothe a poor old hunched-over Appalachian Jew.

So shutting down early had crossed her mind, because a feeling was creeping up from the soles of her feet that tonight was going to be a doozy. It was almost like the Earth itself was sending up bad vibes, that the billion-year-old rocks and mud of the world's oldest mountains sensed something unclean was walking over them.

If tonight was going to be a doozy, and the Horseback

Preacher found his horse, then going home and worming deep under the quilts sounded like a good idea. Dollar or no dollar.

Sarah was closing out the cash register, figuring to turn over the sign on the door (from "Come On In—We're Broke!!!" to "Missed You—And Your Money, too!!!") even though it was only five o'clock. Word had gotten around about her fainting spell, so any regular who dropped by would understand. As for the tourists, like those who rented out the cabins on the hill, let them haul their big white rumps into Titusville and mingle with the Tennessee welfare moms in the Wal-Mart.

She was counting the twenties—not enough of them to suit her—when the screen door *spanged* open and Mark Draper barged in. He'd been a regular since settling in Solom, and Sarah pumped him a time or two about the goings-on at the Smith farm that night. But he clammed up tight about it even when Sarah hinted that they were neighbors now. She could almost admire his attitude if secrecy wasn't so god-danged frustrating.

"Howdy, Mister Draper." She slipped the twenties under the cash register in case he took a notion to rob her. Sheriff Littlefield told her the man had been arrested for drugs, and although he'd behaved himself for the past year, he was obviously capable of killing. Gordon Smith could have testified to that fact.

"You still open?" he asked.

"I'm about to close, but if you need something, go ahead."

Sarah counted out coins, keeping one eye on him as he navigated the aisles, picking up a few canned goods and a loaf of bread. He came back to the counter and laid his groceries by the register, and then selected a Reese's Cup from the candy rack and tossed it down as well.

"Weirdest thing," he said. "I saw horseshoe prints in the

mud by the porch steps."

"People will ride in any kind of weather around here," she said, totaling up the purchases.

"Day or night," he said. "I heard hoof beats at 3 a.m. They woke me up. I thought it was a thunderstorm."

"Was clear last night," Sarah said, noncommittal. "Little bit of moon."

"I looked out the window to check. Through the trees, I could see the river road, shining like a silver ribbon. If I didn't know better, I could have sworn there was a mounted rider herding a pack of goats."

"Sounds like a whale of a dream."

"Sounds like the Horseback Preacher."

Sarah punched the big "Sale" button on the register. The bell rang and the drawer slid open. "That'll be $19.27 with tax."

He held out a twenty. "I know I'm a stranger here, even after a year. But my daughter's here, too, and if there's any kind of danger—"

She snatched the bill away. "I run a trade, Mister Draper. That means something for something. Not something for free."

"I don't get it."

"You don't get nothing until you tell me what happened that night on the Smith farm."

Sarah kept her gaze fixed on him. He took a paper bag from the stack by the register and snapped it open, then began shoveling his goods into it. "You read the papers like everybody else. And I have a feeling you received inside information from the sheriff, as well as the speculation of all of Solom's fine folk. I doubt if the truth is half as colorful as the gossip."

"Try me," she said. "I know Gordon Smith went crazy, but

some folks whisper that the Horseback Preacher was there that night."

"Katy and Jett said so, but I was out of it. Gordon Smith cut me badly with a scythe and I nearly bled out. So I missed the fun part."

"That's odd, considering the sheriff has you down for killing Gordon Smith in self-defense."

"I didn't see the Horseback Preacher that night. All I saw was a scarecrow. One that turned out to be Gordon in his lunatic costume."

"Fair enough. I seen the Horseback Preacher myself, here in the store, just the other day. And again last night. Your girl and her mom were here, too."

His eyes grew distant. "She didn't tell me..."

"Because you're not part of this. It's Solom's mess. You were just an innocent bystander that got drug into it last time, but now you'd best just go back to your cabin and stay there for a while. Might be wise to lay low until old Harmon Smith heads off into the dark toward his next stop."

"Not while my daughter's in danger."

"Suit yourself. But I can't help you."

He reached across the counter, grabbing for her sweater. She stepped back just as the little bell over the door rang. Sue Norwood entered the store, a rock climber's pick-ax in her hand.

"Are you okay?" Sue asked Sarah, lifting the pick-ax as if she knew how to use it.

Mark raised his hands, palms showing in a submissive gesture. He snatched up his sack of groceries. "I was just leaving."

Sue looked at Sarah, who nodded. Sarah was bone tired, eighty years of standing up to gravity and worry and fright finally coming down square on her shoulders. Who cared if

Harmon swooped in and reaped her? One less Jewish shopkeeper in the world wouldn't make a damn bit of difference in the big scheme of things.

"Mister Draper?" Sarah said.

He turned back to her, his eyes smoldering with hidden thoughts.

"Your change." She held out the coins and he took them. Then he shoved past Sue and head outside.

"What was that all about?" Sue said.

"Somebody sticking their nose where it didn't belong."

"If he stays, he'll end up loving it here."

"I got a feeling he's making a play for his ex-wife," Sarah said. "He seems like that sort of romantic fool. He acts like he's hanging around for his daughter's sake, but I seen the way he looks at Katy."

Sue grinned at her. "Sounds like somebody else is sticking their nose where it don't belong."

"It's my town. I keep up with things."

"This is my town, too," Sue said. "And I'm ready to fight for it. I'm going after the Horseback Preacher."

"You and everybody else," Sarah said. Though she had a feeling they wouldn't have to do much seeking.

"There's just one thing about this," Sarah said.

"Whatever," Sue said, still clutching the climber's pick-ax. "I'm already nuts to believe any of this, so just lay it all out."

"The Horseback Preacher only takes one. He had his shot at me, and I didn't cut the mustard with him for whatever reason. Not that I'm complaining, but I don't know if I want to double my odds. And it may be that he's ready to take on outsiders like you. After all, a soul's a soul, no matter where it come from."

"I'll take my chances. I worked too hard to get established here. I'm not going to run off without a fight."

"That's a lot of gumption for a little thing like you. But that pick-ax might not do any good against a dead guy."

Sue swung the pick-ax handle against her other palm and it caught it with a smack. "It feels right, somehow. Like you're supposed to use something that's part of who you are."

"In that case," Sarah said. She rummaged under the counter and brought out the twenty-gauge shotgun. She broke down the barrel and checked the shell. The gun hadn't been fired in five years but the powder had been kept dry. She reached up on the shelves behind her where she displayed ammunition for sale. Pulling down a box of bird-shot shells, she opened it and slipped three of them in her pants pocket.

"If I need more than three shots, the last one is for me," she said, pointing her thumb to her chin to show she'd blow her own head off before she let the Horseback Preacher gallop her soul off to hell. Except part of her wondered if, by committing such an act, she would be volunteering to play the part of victim.

"So how come you're ready to take on this creature now, after you've lived with it for eighty years?" Sue asked.

"Because I'm dog tired of being scared. I don't have many years left, but I'd like to be able to sleep with both eyes shut when I finally hit my deathbed for good. What about *you*?"

Sue shrugged. "I have it good here. I don't want to lose it. Sometimes that's enough."

"Well, maybe this is the generation that breaks the circuit. I wouldn't mind having that as a legacy."

They stood looking at each other for a moment, sheepish expressions on their faces. "What now?" Sue asked.

"You got your Jeep?"

"It's by the shop."

"Let's take a ride, then."

"Where?"

"If you want to catch a mouse, you have to think like a mouse. If you want to catch a contrary preacher that's a hundred-and-fifty years dead and won't accept it, then you have to think like one of those, too. And if I was the Horseback Preacher, I'd head for high ground."

"High ground? You mean Lost Ridge?"

"Can't think of any better place for a soul to get lost, can you?"

"I'm not sure he has a soul."

"Turn over the sign on the door and I'll close out the register. If there's a chance I'm dying tonight, I don't want some Yankee lawyer claiming the petty cash as part of my estate."

"You're a woman after my own heart," Sue said.

"Except I ain't got one."

CHAPTER THIRTY-FIVE

"Maybe we should call Dad," Jett said.

"No way am I dragging him into this," Katy said.

"Can you just drop your pride for a half a sec? I see the way you look at him."

"It's not that simple, honey. There's so much baggage—"

"He's clean now. Both of us are. I know you're not a Bible beater, but don't you believe in second chances? Even for yourself?"

"I've already had two chances. One ex-husband and one dead husband."

"Do you still love him?"

"It's complicated."

"What can be less complicated than that? It's the easiest pass-fail test in the world. I mean, I am one hundred percent sure I don't love Tommy Wilson."

"I don't need the drama right now."

"Our goats are trying to eat our asses, this Horseback Preacher thing is back from the grave, and the people of Solom say everybody he kills comes back sooner or later. That means good old Gordy may shamble back from the grave and try to finish the job. I don't think a little extra drama would even get noticed at this point."

As the afternoon sun sank lower, they'd pretended to go through ordinary routines, eating lunch, reading, and even wasting time watching a dumb science fiction movie in which radioactive spiders swelled to the size of Volkswagen Beetles. In fact, Katy was pretty sure she'd glimpsed such a vehicle beneath one of the oversize, mutant arachnids.

But now, with the sun reaching the ridges and spreading a red blanket across the valley, Katy didn't know how they would fake it through another night.

"Maybe we should leave for a while," Katy said.

"What? After all your talk about sticking it out and refusing to lose? How you weren't going to let bad memories drive you away from the one place where you maybe belonged? Don't tell me we went through all the Gordon crap and police crap and court crap and now you're ready to just give up the farm?"

"We'll still have the strongest legal claim to it."

"Yeah, right. You've been bitching about not having any savings left, and good old Gordon spent all his money on researching mountain religions, which puts me in real good shape for college. You may not have noticed, but not everything's about you. Or do I need to say 'We'll get through it together' one more time?"

Katy was surprised by Jett's outburst. The stress had been building for weeks despite their little fantasy of a quiet farm life, as if they both sensed a malevolent energy in the air. "Okay, okay," she said. "Why don't we just get out of town for a few days? The chickens will be okay, and we'll get Odus to round up the goats later."

IF there's a later.

"Why don't we just stay at Dad's?"

"Because he's in Solom now. I'll call my mom. A few days of Florida sunshine won't kill us and your grades are strong enough that you can afford to miss school."

"Unless those zombie land sharks and sewer-pipe pythons decide to have a party. Can't be worse than here, though."

"Okay, pack and meet me at the car," Katy said. "But hurry. I get the feeling we want to be out of Solom before sundown. I'll call Mom and Mark and tell them our plans."

Katy's mom was delighted to hear from her, especially when she found out she'd be getting her granddaughter as a bonus prize. Mark, however, was guarded.

"I don't see why you need to leave," Mark said on the phone. "You said yourself that hanging in there was the best way to protect your claim to the property. From what I hear around here, the court system is pretty much a good-old-boy's network and they'll look for any chance to turn it back over to the Smith family. I'm lucky they haven't filed a wrongful-death suit against me even though I nearly got my neck chopped off by that maniac."

"I can handle good old boys," Katy said. "What I can't handle is all this talk of killer goats. And the Horseback Preacher. We all saw him at the general store."

"I saw him, too—in the middle of the night. But I believe it's just another act, like Gordon dressing up in his scarecrow outfit. I think these people love their legends so much they keep them alive however they can."

"He's real, Mark. He saved us from Gordon last year. But I don't think he really cared about us. It was more like he was punishing Gordon and we weren't even there."

"Yeah, yeah. Because you're not part of Solom. I've heard the same stories as you."

"It doesn't matter. We're leaving."

"Katy—"

"I'll have Jett call you from the road. Bye."

She wasn't sure if she was being unreasonable or just refusing to let Mark influence her life. Or maybe she simply refused to believe this was happening, despite her own encounters with Solom's supernatural legends. In the cold light of day, it was easy to think Gordon's attack and the Harmon Smith's sudden materialization had been nothing but a fantasy, but on long autumn nights, the legends seemed all too real.

Katy made sure the yard was clear before she hauled her overnight bag to the Subaru. She flung the bag in the hatchback and closed it, then got behind the wheel and tapped it impatiently, glancing around to make sure no goats returned. Jett slid into the passenger seat a minute later, dropping her shoulder bag in the floor between her feet.

"Did you lock up?" Katy asked.

"Yep. Wouldn't want anybody stealing your...wait, you don't have anything."

Katy adjusted the rearview mirror and froze.

In the backseat was the female scarecrow from the barn. Its cheesecloth head was missing.

But Rebecca's voice chilled her even more: *"It's time to go."*

Jett jumped out of the car. "Holy crap, Mom. Did you hear that?"

Katy harbored no desire to say "Told you so." Even though she'd accepted the ghost's existence, the encounter caused her hair follicles to tingle and heart to race. But Rebecca's calm delivery kept her from fleeing the car. Instead, curiosity won out.

After all, they'd shared a husband and shared a house for more than a year. They were practically sisters.

"Go where?" Katy asked the scarecrow figure.

"Mom," Jett said, backing away. "You're...talking to her?"

"We have a history," Katy said. She repeated her question to the back seat. Then Rebecca appeared beside the scarecrow, with milky skin, big black eyes, long dark hair, and a wicked gash around her neck.

The ghost said, *"Listen to me if you want to live."*

CHAPTER THIRTY-SIX

Odus reached the ridge line and dismounted, letting Sister Mary nibble some dried-up rabbit tobacco as he scanned the granite boulders and stunted cedars that the wind had swept for ages. The path narrowed and grew rougher, used mostly by foxes, the occasional black bear, and deer.

Yet this would have been the way Harmon Smith would have crossed to Virginia or eastern Tennessee. The valley cut through gaps at each end of Lost Ridge that would have resulted in less of a climb, but they were each nearly ten miles out of the way. A car had no trouble with the extra distance, and the state highway department stuck as close to the lower elevations as possible. But Harmon Smith had ridden in the days before highways and still marched to the echo of that long-dead era.

Odus expected some sign, a hoof print or a broken tree branch or maybe even Old Saint's spoor, whatever that might look like. But all he'd found were crackling leaves, hardwoods damaged by acid rain and insects, and the cold October air at 4,500 feet of altitude. He'd spooked a few ravens, and a red hawk cut an arc in the violet sky before diving for some unlucky rodent, but the forest remained quiet. He went for the whiskey bottle again, letting the Old Crow warm his tongue.

"Looks like I took us on a wild goose chase," he said to the horse. Sister Mary flicked her mane out of her eyes as if nodding in agreement.

Odus heard a clattering, like the sound of wood against stone. Or the clop of a horse's hoof.

"You've come a long way," came a voice from the thinning trees. "Seek and you shall find, knock and the door shall be opened."

"I *do* want something," Odus said, in the general direction of the voice. He would never forget the cold, deep tones of the Horseback Preacher. Outside, the voice seemed to boom even more than it had inside the general store. "I want this to be over. I want *you* to be over."

"Come to me, all that are weary and carrying heavy burdens, and I will give you rest."

"The folks that are alive today didn't have anything to do with what happened to you. Why don't you just go on and leave us in peace?"

"I desire mercy, not sacrifice."

An unseen horse whinnied. The laurel branches quivered, parted, and the horse stepped out, black with a pure white chest the way the legends described him. He stood a good head taller than Sister Mary, whose ears twitched at the sight of the animal. The Horseback Preacher was astride his horse, sitting tall in the saddle, head tilted down.

Even looking up at him from below, Odus had a hard time distinguishing his features. The dying sunlight was at the Horseback Preacher's back, the sky cast purple with shredded sheets of pink. The shadows of the trees seemed to grow up from the ground and enshroud the mounted figure.

Odus wondered if this was the showdown he'd been seeking. Maybe he was supposed to jump on Sister Mary, ride hell-bent for leather toward the dead preacher, and tangle with him head-on. If he'd brought a firearm, he probably would have faced him down like a tin-star hero.

"We're not the ones who killed you," Odus said.

"You belong to Solom. That's reason enough."

"It ain't the *place* that sinned. It was just a few preachers who did you in, the way I hear it. And they're dead. They faced their judgment long ago, before Him that has power over all of us."

The Horseback Preacher's head lifted, and Odus recognized that strong, jowly Smith chin. The hidden eyes suddenly flared like a campfire's embers urged by the wind. "You think I like making these rounds? You think I have a choice? Did you ever consider maybe something's got power over *me*? For the Bible says, 'If you are forced to go one mile, go also the second.'"

Odus gripped the dangling reins and held Sister Mary's head tight. The pinto tried to back away, but the terrain was too rough and dangerous. A stench drifted off the Horseback Preacher, the smell of a dead skunk in the road, but a whisk of wind carried it off, leaving only the strong, green smell of pine and the earthy aroma of fallen and decaying leaves.

"I've come to stop you," Odus said.

"I wish you could," the Horseback Preacher said, relaxing his pale hands and patting his horse on the neck. "Narrow is the gate and hard is the road that leads to life, and there are few who find it."

"Why don't you just step down off that saddle, hang up your hat, and let it go?"

"Told you, I got a mission. I didn't ask for it. It was given to me."

"I don't believe in the Devil."

"Neither do I, Mr. Odus Hampton." The Horseback Preacher leaned to one side and spat, as if ridding himself of many years of bitter trail dust. "I knew your daddy. Good man. I could have taken him in the summer of '77, when he was up on a ladder cleaning out gutters on the Smith House."

"He worked for Gordon's daddy."

"And you worked for Gordon. Some things don't change

in Solom."

"I reckon one thing's going to have to change."

"Not tonight. Not here and now, between you and me."

"I'm afraid so, mister." Odus's throat was dry, but he wouldn't let his voice weaken or crack.

"Who do you think brought you here? Don't tell me you woke up this morning and it just popped into your head to steal a horse and ride to the top of Lost Ridge."

"I did some studying on it first."

"That's the trouble with you folks. You think you're the boss of your arms and legs and mind, you think your soul is separate and free from your flesh. And I'm here to tell you otherwise."

The chill that crept over Odus's skin had only a little to do with the day's fading warmth. As the sky grew darker, the shadows around Harmon Smith lessened, as if the man was absorbing the blackness. More of his face was visible, and the meat over his jaws looked to be the texture of crumbling wax. Old Saint stood stock-still during their conversation, while Sister Mary pawed the ground, shuffled, and snorted in dismay.

Odus noted that maybe being dead had its advantages when it came to the equestrian arts. No saddle sores.

"Well, I found you, so that means there's a reason, doesn't it?" Odus ached for a shot of whiskey, but then wondered if the ache was due to his own need or was caused by the whim of some bearded guy behind the clouds. He had little use for religion, but, like most hopeless sinners, he wrapped his hands around it when it was the only rope available for climbing out of a dark pit.

"You're not special, you're just early," the Horseback Preacher said.

Confused, Odus figured he'd best keep the creature

talking while he came up with a plan. "Did you kill them two tourists on the Switchback Trail? You're only supposed to kill one and then be one your way. That's how it's always been, as far back as they remember to tell it. I thought you held with tradition."

"Know them by their fruits."

"You're evil. How can a man of the cloth go around killing like that?" Odus was casting about for a fallen tree branch or a loose jag of granite. He felt foolish now for not bringing a gun. He still wasn't sure what sort of weapon would work, if any. His was a mission of faith, despite the Horseback Preacher's mocking.

The Horseback Preacher ran a gaunt, crooked finger through a hole in his jacket. "Cloth is like flesh, it goes to worms. The spirit is the thing that doesn't die."

The Horseback Preacher lifted his head and glanced above them through a gap in the canopy, his mouth curling up at one corner. A beech leaf spiraled down from the twisted branches and fluttered across his face. The woods were hushed in that moment as the birds and wildlife changed shifts, the daytime animals settling into holes, nests, and protective crooks of tree limbs while the nocturnal creatures roused from the slumber.

The silence was disturbed by a faint buzzing from below, as if a giant nest of hornets had been stirred with a stick. Harmon Smith's cracked lips bent like a snake with a broken spine in something that might have been a smile if seen on a human face.

"I suppose the others got the same idea you did," he said. "Funny how you give them a choice and they make the wrong one every single time. Few find the true way."

The buzz grew louder, changed into a roar. It was a vehicle engine. Somebody was climbing the rough logging roads that crisscrossed the mountain. And those roads led to the top, where Odus stared down his adversary. His brow furrowed in doubt. He was supposed to do this alone, wasn't he?

At that moment, Sister Mary reared, flailing her forelegs in front of her, stripping the leather reins through Odus's palm, cutting into his flesh. She broke and galloped into the trees, neck stooped low and ears pinned close to her head.

The Horseback Preacher stroked Old Saint's mane, and the revenant horse chuckled softly in response. "I guess your friend there just exercised her free will, huh?"

Odus took two steps backward, toward the rocky ledge that led to one of the logging roads. It was a thirty-foot drop. He could try to climb down, but he pictured his fingers gripping the granite ledge and Old Saint bringing a heavy, scarred hoof down on them. He could follow Sister Mary and blaze a trail through the tangles, or he could stand his ground and see what God had in store for him.

None of the options settled the squirming in his chest and gut. The courage that had surged through him since this morning now seemed foolish and silly. He possessed no special gifts or weapons to bring to bear against a supernatural creature. He'd fallen back onto a sort of crippled faith, believing God would provide in Odus's hour of need. But Odus didn't consider that he'd never been a deeply religious man, or that faith couldn't be turned off and on like tap water.

"You fear me, but only because you don't understand me," the Horseback Preacher said, over the increasing roar of the engine. "If the shepherd has one hundred sheep, and one of them goes astray, does he not leave the other ninety-nine on the mountains and go in search of the one that went astray?"

The Horseback Preacher wheeled his mount and trotted

back through the laurel thicket. The branches shook from his passage as if horse and rider were as solid and real as any living creature. But the smell of decay lingered, a smell that hinted of grave dirt and spent fires and blood dried black.

CHAPTER THIRTY-SEVEN

A chauffeur for the dead.

Katy guided the Subaru off the highway onto the old logging road, sure that the last bit of sanity had slipped from her, leaving the nerves of her brain raw and exposed.

Why else would she be taking directions from a ghost? Her instinct was to stay on the highway and make time to Florida, maybe stopping at a Holiday Inn halfway between. Anything that would have put distance between Jett and Solom.

But Rebecca's lost voice connected with her on some primal, feminine level. They were two women who had traveled the same path, though Rebecca's had ended too early and violently.

Jett was reluctant to get back in the car after Rebecca had warned them of what was underway that night: Gordon had returned to the farm and retrieved the other scarecrow. Katy almost said, "But he's dead," and then realized such distinctions didn't matter in Solom. She also remembered something Sarah Jeffers had warned her about. Whoever the Horseback Preacher takes always comes back.

"Well, Mom, this is just great," Jett said. "You brought me to Solom to get me off drugs and then you drop me right into the biggest bad-acid trip in the universe."

"Just hang on, honey," Katy said. She glanced in the rearview. Rebecca was gone but her words came as if she were leaning over the seat: *Up the mountain.*

Up, an ascension, as if the journey bore a spiritual as well as physical element. But didn't all journeys? If you thought of life as a road that must be traveled, then you encountered all kinds of exit ramps, signal lights, pit stops, and, eventually, a vehicle breakdown.

Each fork was an opportunity, as the poet Robert Frost pointed out, but no one ever figured out if each road taken was a choice or an obligation. If you took the road less traveled, was it because you wanted to, or because you were compelled?

Katy decided this road was definitely the one less traveled, because the Subaru bottomed out in the ruts, the arcs of the headlights bouncing ahead like light sabers cutting a path through the wilderness. The car was all-wheel drive, which gave it enough traction to navigate the roughest parts of the old road, but it groaned in protest as it leaped and jittered.

"Mom, what are we supposed to do when we get there?"

"I don't think we're supposed to know," Katy said.

"*You just have to get there,*" Rebecca said, suddenly whole again, or the closest she could come to that corporeal state.

Jett jerked away, sitting forward in her seat, fighting the tension of the seat belt. "Hey! Don't do that. You're freaking me out enough already without popping out of thin air."

"*I'm a ghost,*" Rebecca said. "*What else do you expect me to do?*"

"I foresee years of therapy ahead," Jett said.

"Just imagine the stories you'll have to tell your grandkids," Katy said, wrestling the steering wheel as the car lurched over a fallen sapling.

"If I live that long. Let's not take that for granted yet. We're on a place called 'Lost Ridge' with a headless woman in the back seat, headed for a showdown with your dead husband and a preacher who has returned from the grave. What could possibly go wrong?"

"They're waiting," Rebecca said.

"They?" Katy asked.

"The ones who are supposed to be there."

"What's with the riddles?" Jett said. "If you know what's going to happen, why don't you tell us?"

"You already know, too. That's the trouble with the living. They only hear the past when they should be listening to the future."

"Oh, great. Mom, you got any dope on you? I can't handle this."

Katy looked at her daughter, whose face was pale green from the interior lights. Her dyed-black bangs were parted, making her look younger than her fifteen years. Yet Katy's little Gothling was knocking on the door to womanhood and all the crazy mysteries waiting ahead. Not to mention the crazy mysteries in the back seat. "You promised, remember?"

"Yeah, yeah." Jett sighed and reached to turn up the music, then changed her mind and settled back against her seat, still leaning away from Rebecca. But she said to the ghost, "So, why did Gordon kill you?"

"Because he loved me. Why else would you kill someone?"

"No," Katy said. "I think the reason is even more selfish that."

As she compelled the Subaru up the logging road, she thought back to Gordon's fascination with myths and old cultures and his ranting about harvest gods and goddesses. Gordon might have thought offering human sacrifice was the most natural thing in the world. Maybe he viewed it as a pleasant little appeasement ritual that had been too long neglected, its neglect bringing about the sorry state of the modern environment. Maybe he was trying to follow in the footsteps of his forefather, Harmon Smith, in observing his own peculiar belief system.

Katy assumed the Horseback Preacher rejected Gordon's

sacrifice last year, when he'd tried to kill her and Jett. But what if the sacrifice had been noted and *rewarded*? What if Gordon was now the preacher's right-hand man in whatever sinister business was now afoot?

Katy shivered and looked through the windshield at the rutted road ahead, wondering what sort of god would compel a man to slaughter his wife and maybe others. Surely Katy and Jett would have been next, and would join Rebecca in haunting the old wooden-frame farmhouse until the end of time.

"He did it because it was his destiny," Katy said, raising her voice over the roar of the straining engine.

"You're freaking me out, Mom," Jett said.

"*Destiny*," Rebecca said. "*That's as good a name for it as any.*"

"So, what's your deal?" Jett said to the ghost. "Are you stuck here or something? Why don't you get to go to heaven or wherever?"

"*I belong to Solom now.*"

"Mom, maybe we'd better find a place to turn around. I don't think I want to die here. It would be a real bitch to be stuck in Solom forever."

"We're not going to die," Katy said.

"The Horseback Preacher might have other ideas."

CHAPTER THIRTY-EIGHT

Alex had a passing knowledge of tracking and hunting, and although he was mostly a vegetarian, he figured being able to round up meat for the dinner table might be a handy survival skill when the Republicans and Democrats finally toppled the Statue of Liberty.

So he'd learned the basics, and had even killed some small game with his bow and arrows. Of course, he was a crack marksman. That was required of any member of the anti-government militia, even if you were only an army of one.

So Alex encountered no trouble following the goats' hoof prints through the woods. Even his sister, a Boston lawyer, could have followed this trail—the fuzzy beasts had practically trampled a superhighway through the underbrush. The carpet of leaves on the forest floor was scuffled, branches hung broken and nibbled, and of course there was the occasional pile of plum-sized goat turds. In his haste, Alex hadn't paid close attention to the ammunition he'd loaded into his shoulder bag, but he figured he carried at least six rounds for each of the goats. Plenty enough lead to teach the Satan-faced little fucks not to mess with *his* property.

The trail followed the ridge. Wherever they were going, they were making a beeline for high ground. Alex understood the chemical processes by which marijuana played with the synapses. Marijuana required heat before the cannabinoids were activated, so you had to smoke it or cook it in brownies or oil for the pot to do its stuff.

But maybe goat neurology was different. Maybe goats

could get stoned just from the raw green leaves. That seemed to be the only reason they would break into his shed and gobble up good bud that would net twenty grand on the street.

Unless they were smart enough to know what the pot meant to him.

Maybe they were part of some secret government experiment, too. He'd read about how the spooks trained dolphins to carry explosives toward enemy ships and trained chimpanzees to infiltrate bunkers. No doubt the government was going gangbusters in their underground labs, splicing all kinds of stuff together, putting microchips in the heads of animals, developing entire battalions of remote-controlled killers.

Alex stopped and adjusted the strap of the submachine gun, the Pearson Freedom bow tucked under his armpit. Maybe the goats were fucking with him on purpose. Maybe they were trying to ... well, to get his goat. The FBI had found out about his stash and his weapons and his tax evasion, and instead of coming up and knocking on the front door with a warrant, they'd concocted the most screwed-up, expensive, and outlandish revenge possible. Yeah, that was what the U.S. of A. was all about.

Well, revenge worked two ways. Alex patted the Colt Python at his side. The ripped-up ground was moist, the mounds of goat shit fresher as he climbed the slope of Lost Ridge. He was gaining on them, even with darkness settling in. And if the universe was as just and fair as Alex always believed it was, especially while brain-basted on a thumb-sized joint of God-green smoke, then he'd have his revenge before the sun surrendered to the night.

Maybe Weird Dude was some sort of upper-level federal agent, in the National Security Agency, even. Shadow Ops at its most devious. The Establishment. Alex realized maybe that particular line of paranoid delusion was probably a bit too extravagant, but it pleased him nonetheless.

An engine roared in the distance and more headlights bobbed in the valley below. Probably the SEALS. He expected choppers at any minute. He'd better get this mission finished before reinforcements arrived.

Alex shifted into a double-time jog, eager to catch up with whatever was awaiting him at the top of the ridge.

CHAPTER THIRTY-NINE

Odus thrashed through the laurels, calling for Sister Mary.

He was mostly sober now, the braving effects of the Old Crow dissipated, leaving in its place a painful veil of fog. Some shining knight he'd made, some backwoods hero. His image of a tin-star stud riding into a dirty town with six-guns blazing was reduced to a hung-over hillbilly who'd lost his ride.

The autumn darkness didn't settle over the sky so much as it seeped up from the cool, ancient mountains. The black stuff of night had crawled around the rude and rounded chunks of granite, out from between the roots of old-growth ash and beech and hickory, up from the hidden holes in world.

Now it knitted its single, all-consuming color in a smothering strait jacket, there at every turn, ready to match every breath, flowing into Odus's lungs and claiming its rightful space. Odus had never felt so much like an invader on this planet as he did now. In fact, he'd never given it any thought at all.

He'd hunted these peaks, sought squirrels and wild turkey and the occasional black bear, but he'd always come here as a conqueror. Now, entangled in its inky depths, his bearings lost, he recognized the futility of laying claim to something as old as the Appalachians.

No human owned these mountains. If anything held deed to these stony and storied lands, it was creatures like the Horseback Preacher, those not bound by time and space and the sad, small worries of the mortal.

Unseen branches tore Odus's hands and waxy leaves slapped his face. He rested for a moment, squinting through the canopy to the scattered stars and the comforting cast of moonlight above.

"God, if you're up there, now would be a great time to lend a little hand here," Odus said, the prayer sounding stupid even as it left his lips. Why should God listen to a man who hadn't stepped foot in a church in two decades, who hadn't cracked a Bible since Sunday school in Free Will Baptist church, who hadn't felt a single spiritual twitch since the day Preacher Blackburn dipped his head into the chilling waters of Rush Branch and pronounced him washed free of sin?

However, his prayer may have been answered, or at least coincided with an earthly event, which amounted to the same thing when you dropped the fancy cloth and got down to brass tacks.

Needles of light broke through the branches ahead. This light was filtered by the leaves, but was a solid force, pushing at the suffocating darkness and promising hope. Odus worked toward it, his footing more sure now as he could make out the black lines of trees and didn't have to feel his way through the vegetative maze.

He heard voices as the light grew stronger, and he recognized one of them: Sarah from the general store. What business did a seventy-year-old woman have on top of Lost Ridge at this time of night? Of course, Odus could ask himself the same question, and maybe the same answer would serve for both of them.

"Hello," he shouted through the trees.

"Who's there?" Sarah said, her voice snapping like a soggy twig.

"Odus."

"Well, come on out of there and count your blessings that I

didn't let loose with some buckshot first. It ain't wise to go sneaking up on a lady in the dark."

"I wasn't sneaking, I was walking," he said.

"Is this your horse, then?" came another voice, and Odus placed it as belonging to Sue Norwood.

Guided by their voices and the intensifying glare of car headlights, Odus threaded through the edge of the laurel thicket and stood in a little clearing at the end of a logging road. He stepped into the comforting cone of light and shielded his eyes. Sister Mary stood by the parked Jeep, snorting, head twitching up and down, and Odus couldn't shake the feeling that Sister Mary was laughing at him.

"Well, she's not rightly mine," Odus said. "I kind of appropriated her for a mission."

"See," Sarah said to Sue, who was holding Sister Mary's reins. "I'm not the only one who's been touched in the head. The whole blamed place goes crazy whenever Harmon Smith rides into town."

"It seemed like the thing to do at the time," Odus said. "I mean, when you hear a higher calling, do you stop and ask questions, or do you just follow that voice?"

"You follow it," Sue said, and Odus could see the pick-axe in her hand, brandished like a crusader's sword.

"That little pig-sticker won't do a thing against the Horseback Preacher," Odus said, then noted the shotgun cradled across Sarah's arm. "I reckon a 20-gauge won't, either."

"Oh, yeah?" Sarah asked. "And what exactly do you have in your bag of tricks there that's supposed to kill a dead preacher? A Mason jar of holy water? A slingshot and a silver dime? An empty liquor bottle?"

Odus's face flushed. He'd tossed the Old Crow bottle into the hollow of a rotted-out stump, but first he'd briefly considered its potential as a spiritual battle-ax. After all, drinking was practically his religion. Now the idea seemed as silly as Sue's and Sarah's weapons of choice.

"Okay, own up to it, we're poking in the dark with a limp stick," he said. "What now?"

"Wait it out, I reckon," Sarah said. "Harmon crashed our party last night, but I think tonight he's playing host."

"The air feels strange," Sue said. "Like it's carrying a mild electrical charge."

Odus had been so wired with tension his senses honed and focused down to the tight ache in his gut. Having found company, and his horse, he was able to relax enough to draw in the moist night air. The inhalation carried the fragrance of balsam and wet leaves, rich loam and moss, the safe, healing aromas of the high forest.

But beneath that, like a corpse's smell oozing from beneath the undertaker's applied mask of perfume, was a corruption of sulfur and ozone, of decay and a pervasive stink of something that didn't belong. The smell almost projected a physical presence, as if it was lightly stroking his skin, coaxing him into vile acts and thoughts.

"I expect the others will be joining us," Sarah said. "I hear cars in the valley."

"He's leading us here?" Sue said.

"Jesus had his sermon on the Mount," Odus said. "Maybe Harmon's ready for his turn."

Sister Mary stepped forward, onto the stage defined by the headlights, and Sue dropped the reins so the horse could reach Odus. Sister Mary brushed Odus's satchel with her nose, and he unzipped it and brought out an apple. As she munched it with a curious, sideways twist of her jaws, Odus was reminded of the goats and their increasing numbers.

"Flock," he said, dimly recalling material from Sunday

School, when the class leader sold the kids on religion by using coloring books and posters. Jesus was often pictured with a flock of some kind, whether it was sheep, children in robes, or grown-ups whose skin colors were varied enough and in the right proportions to make you think that, sure, black folks could get to heaven, too, only there probably wouldn't be too many of them and God would surely give them a place off to themselves.

The common theme was the gathering of creatures around Jesus, as if the Son of God would get lonely if He didn't have living things milling around him, all waiting for a wise word or a bit of free food.

"Flock what?" Sarah said.

"The goats made me think of it," Odus said. "They've been breeding like rabbits in the past year, especially on the Smith farm. Maybe Harmon Smith wants a flock again, and we're it."

Sarah looked around, as if afraid of what might lurk beyond the false security of the headlights, the shotgun tilted to the ground. "What in the world does he need with *us*? He should have killed somebody and been gone already."

"Maybe he needs something different this time," Odus said. "Notice we both said *need*. Like we got to serve some purpose."

"We?" Sarah said. "You can just leave me out of it."

"He implied others will be coming along shortly," Odus said, realizing how pitiful and small his lone effort seemed, riding into the mountains like a fool.

"Well, we ain't serving nothing by just standing here," Sarah said. "I guess we ought to get this over with. I got work in the morning."

"Where do we look first?" Sue asked.

Odus stroked the lean, sinewy neck of Sister Mary, who

nuzzled against the flannel of his shirt. "I think our animal friend here knows the way."

CHAPTER FORTY

Jett decided her mom was spacing out again, because she seemed calm as she navigated the narrow, rutted road up Lost Ridge.

A couple of times the Subaru swerved over to the ledge and the valley opened up in a dizzying scene below. In those moments of vertigo, Jett covered her eyes and imagined what her obituary would look like. She figured her obit would have the same problem as most: it would be way too short. Plus it would leave out the cool stuff like her love of Robert Smith and The Cure, the night she survived an attacked by her deranged stepdad, and the ghost in the back seat.

The road leveled out and grew wider. Mom steered the car over a grassy area, though a path appeared to have been tattooed into the dirt. Tire tracks cut twin grooves in the open stretch of land, flattening the wet weeds. The tracks were recent.

"Someone's ahead of us," Katy said. "I can see their taillights."

Jett turned to Rebecca, still not quite used to the shock of that ethereal face, the hollow eyes that looked out as if from the bottom of a deep and drowning cave, the thin lips that were as insubstantial as mist.

"What's up?" Jett said to Rebecca.

Jett didn't like the way the torn flesh around the woman's neck rippled as she spoke, as if unearthly air passed through her windpipe. *"We're all on the same path,"* the ghost said.

"Yeah, but what does that mean?"

"It means we have to look," Mom said, turning her head for a moment. "We're part of this. We can't just go off and leave a mystery hanging."

"Sure we can, Mom. Remember the Smith scarecrow? Remember the goats? What do I have to do, die and come back as a ghost myself to get your attention?"

"We can get through this together."

Jett almost choked on the Mom-ism but decided to go with it this time. After all, she had no choice. Even if she jumped out of the car and survived, she'd still be facing a long hike down the mountain. And then what would she do? Call Dad and ask for a lift? Her cell phone wasn't getting any signal back here in the wilds.

Plus Mom had an odd, intense look on her face, and Jett wasn't sure she should be abandoned.

"Rebecca, tell Mom this is crazy," Jett said.

"*This is crazy*," the ghost said, mouth parting to reveal darkness inside the translucent flesh.

"Yes, but we're here," Mom said, applying the brakes. "Looks like the party's just started."

The Subaru emerged from the woods, revealing a clearing of low grass, scrub, and protruding granite boulders, a hillbilly Stonehenge. The man in the black hat sat on a rock, surrounded by goats, while people came walking out of the woods to gather around. Jett recognized some of them: there was Odus, sitting astride a horse; Jerry Bennington, her math teacher, was standing to one side, wearing his bow-tie; the man who lived up the road from the Smith farm and occasionally rumbled by in his battered pick-up was hunched at one edge of the clearing, holding some type of hunting bow and arrow.

There were others from last night's gathering at the general store. Sarah cradled the shotgun across the crook of one knotty elbow. Kim Deister leaned against a boulder, wielding some sort of wicked-looking semiautomatic rifle. Sue Norwood's Jeep bathed the bizarre tableau in light, and as Mom killed the Subaru engine, she left the headlights on and aimed at the rock formation, giving the menagerie a strange, stark radiance.

And in the center of it all stood the Horseback Preacher, hands clasped and head tilted back as if sniffing the sky.

Jett turned to query Rebecca on this weird gathering, but Rebecca was gone. At least, *most* of her was. Her disembodied head hovered in the rear passenger area, slowly fading to thin air. The last to fade were those dark, hollow eyes, and they seemed to hold a challenge and a glimmer of triumph.

"I hate it when she does that," Jett said.

CHAPTER FORTY-ONE

Sarah leveled the shotgun at the Horseback Preacher, who stood with his thin arms spread in welcome.

Four dozen goats knelt before the dead preacher, tranquil and waiting under the glare of the Jeep headlights. That might have been the creepiest part of the whole scene: the Horseback Preacher's eyes burned yellow in the light, his waxen face and gaunt cheeks visible under the wide brim of his black hat, and his smile was like a broken snake under his long, thin nose, but goats were *never* still.

They usually twitched and nattered and stomped and kicked, and most of all, their jaws were always working on something. But these animals folded up before Harmon Smith as if they were dosed with tranquilizers and headed for a long drowse. Even the scruffy young kids among them were motionless and relaxed, scarcely wiggling an ear.

Old Saint was tied to a tree at the edge of the clearing, and it was the first time Sarah had ever seen the fabled creature. He was an admirable hunk of horse flesh, if "flesh" was the right word. He might have been a stack of decades up from the grave, but he looked as solid as the oak that served as his hitching post. The horse nibbled at a patch of moss on the tree, as if he'd already heard the sermon that Harmon Smith appeared about to deliver.

Sue climbed behind the wheel of the Jeep, apparently having second thoughts about her desire to scrub Solom clean of its legends. Odus regained Sister Mary's good graces and sat astride the paint pony to the left of the Jeep. The young man who held some sort of bow-and-arrow stood on the opposite side of the clearing, as if he'd wound through the woods on foot.

Sarah recognized him from a couple of his shopping trips to the store, where he bought only cheap staples like rice and dried beans. It was no coincidence that the man had shown up here at the same time as her little trio, and she suffered no doubt that the reason for their mutual summoning was buried in the supernatural skullspace beneath that ragged-rimmed black hat over there.

If the Horseback Preacher even *had* a brain, that was. Sarah suspected if that skull was laid open with a shotgun blast, it would ooze a stinky, sticky tar. The juice of madness and evil, the sort of stuff that might pump through Satan's icy hot veins.

She was tempted to give Harmon Smith a load of birdshot, just to test the waters, so to speak, but she sensed the stage wasn't completely set yet. Harmon had a few other pieces to move into the picture, and he seemed in no particular hurry, as if a full-moon October Sunday night was just the right time for a nice, peaceful gathering of his congregation.

"Shoot him, Sarah," Sue said from the Jeep's cab.

"You don't just up and shoot a man without giving him a chance to explain himself," Sarah said, keeping the fright out of her voice. "Otherwise the gender would have been wiped out ages ago. Besides, sometimes it's fun to hear a man open his mouth just to hear what kind of lie comes out."

"Come hear my truth," Harmon shouted, although he was too far away to have heard Sarah, just at the edge of effective shotgun range. But he looked to be in range of the man with the cocked arrow, who raised his own weapon. Other weapons were slung over his shoulder, and he sported a sidearm in a belt holster.

"Do these shitbag animals belong to you?" the archer asked the Horseback Preacher, voice trembling with either fear or anger.

Harmon swept out a casual hand to indicate the ridge and the valley below. "All this belongs to me," the preacher answered. "And other places as well. My road is long and my service has been longer."

"Drop the double-talk, Weird Dude," the man said. "If these are yours, you've got reparations to pay. Because you trespassed against me."

"Fences are for the living, Alex Eakins. I go where I want because Solom belongs to me. I'm beyond boundaries."

Sarah thought the man, Alex Eakins, looked to have an itchy release finger on his notched arrow. "My deed is registered at the courthouse," he said.

"And mine is recorded in the Book of Knowledge."

"Are you with the government?"

"I answer to one law."

"What's with the riddles, man?" Alex raised his voice, addressing Sarah, Sue, and Odus. "What's everybody doing up here?"

"We're here for the same reason you are," Sarah said.

"To kill some damned goats?"

"They came because of me," the Horseback Preacher said. "As did all my creatures."

"Hey, dude, I saw those goats *eating* you."

"I provide nourishment to my flock."

Sarah figured Harmon Smith, back when he was alive, had been touched in the head somewhere along the line, around the time he traded in his Methodist leanings for a belief in fleshly sacrifice. After all those years roaming the back woods to visit various Appalachian communities, killing somebody here and there along the way, he'd probably made peace with his madness.

"I have a message to deliver," Harmon Smith said, as if he'd looked inside Sarah's head. He drew his ragged wool coat about him with gaunt fingers. "But we'll have to wait for the others."

"Others?" Odus said.

At that moment, Sarah heard a mechanical roar rising from the slopes below and echoing in the cup of the valley. Cars, at least three and maybe more, the rumble of a convoy as the engines whined against the climb. She wondered how many the Horseback Preacher would summon tonight.

Harmon Smith sat on the rock in his yoga position, the snake of a smile bending into a deeper smirk. "My flock," he said. "All my lovely creatures."

CHAPTER FORTY-TWO

Odus gripped the reins to steady Sister Mary as more people came out from the trees, vehicles groaned up the old logging roads of Lost Ridge, and a few stray goats staggered into the combined glare of half a dozen headlights. It was like some kind of bizarre revival service, with the Horseback Preacher summoning a great congregation.

Odus couldn't finish the job. It was too big for him. He was unworthy. He was just a drunk who couldn't hold down a steady job, a dirty horse thief, part of a bloodline that had squatted on these lands since Colonial times without really improving them.

The Eakins boy, the one who owned a piece of property above the Smith place, stood with a taut bow, unsure of which direction to aim his arrow. Loretta Whitley and her son Todd each held pitchforks, looking like frightened members of a mob storming Victor Frankenstein's castle. Amos Clayton sported a shotgun of a larger bore than Sarah's, although he seemed uncertain about using it. Kim Deister handled her weapon as if she was dead certain to spill blood.

Odus wondered if they each suffered the same delusion, of being called to kill the Horseback Preacher and finally lay the preacher to rest, bringing peace to the valley. Or perhaps they'd come to offer themselves on the altar of life. Regardless, many heeded the call.

Several more vehicles rolled into the clearing, and the smell of exhaust briefly muted the stench of the goats and the bright metallic odor of human fear. Odus recognized Claude

Tester's Ford pick-up, and a sport utility vehicle pulled up beside it. A Sheriff's Department patrol car, a Crown Victoria, had been beaten up by the rough road, but the front-wheel drive dragged the car to the peak.

The door on the patrol car opened and a deputy stepped out, half his face blotted by a red birthmark, one hand on his sidearm. Odus figured the deputy would try to take control and restore order, but he seemed as much under the Horseback Preacher's sway as the rest of them.

"Welcome, all," the preacher said, standing on legs that unfolded like broken black sticks. In the fuzzy aura of headlights, he seemed almost a silhouette in his moth-eaten black suit. He lifted the brim of his hat and turned in a semicircle so that all the assembled could see his face. The skin was as smooth as hardened wax, and just as brittle. The preacher's eyes were the bloodied color of a harvest moon just after sundown.

The crowd fell silent, as if each word might be the one that delivered the Truth. The late-arriving goats joined their kind near the flat stone that served as the Horseback Preacher's pulpit, and they, too, settled into passive and meek positions.

The people who emerged from the woods—Odus saw Marletta Hoyle, the wispy-haired English teacher at the elementary school, carrying an eagle-head cane as if she meant to brain Harmon Smith like a wayward student—drew closer around the stone with an air of expectation.

"We're not all here yet," the Horseback Preacher said. "Soon."

A man concealed in the safety of the forest called out, "Go back to where you come from, you black devil."

The Horseback Preacher grinned, showing teeth as orange as candy corn. "This *is* where I came from."

The unseen man hollered, "You wasn't born to Solom. The

damned Methodists sent you."

"It was a Methodist who rode into this fair valley all those years ago," he said, in a voice that would make any preacher, living or dead, proud. "But that Methodist found other, older ways here. The ways of the harvest."

"We're God-fearing folk, Harmon Smith," Loretta Whitley said, slamming the point of her pitchfork handle into the ground for emphasis. "Why don't you go on about your business and leave us alone?"

"This is my business," the Horseback Preacher said. "Just as God ordered Abraham to lay his own son on the altar, so did the people of Solom listen when God commanded them to slay me."

"If God wanted you, why didn't he take you?" Sarah shouted, surprising Odus with the strength in her voice. "Why do you keep coming back and killing?"

The Horseback Preacher laughed, a sound as raw as an owl's screech and as deep as the howling of a red wolf. "We all serve a purpose under God's sky. The tree is known by its fruits."

"What about your goats, Weird Dude?" asked the Eakins boy. The way his hands were trembling, Odus figured the arrow would let fly any second. Maybe all of them were waiting to see who would attack Harmon Smith first. Then they could all join in with whatever weapons or talismans they had brought.

Odus realized he still hadn't decided on a weapon. He trusted that the way would be shown, but now that the moment was at hand, no voice from the wilderness gave him instruction. Through all his false courage, he was alone. As they all were, despite their number.

"Which one of us do you want, Harmon?" Claude Tester called. "We know you need to take one of us, and we know you've done passed over a few."

"I want all of you," the Horseback Preacher said. "Why do you think I keep returning?"

"You're just a pesky old buzzard," Sarah said with a rush of courage. "You pick at the bones of the past. But we don't need you around no more."

"It's not about what you need, Sarah Jeffers. It's about what's meant to be."

"Well, I ain't meant to be standing on the top of a cold mountain in the middle of an October night, what with my arthritis flaring up."

"You're here, though, aren't you?"

Sarah had no answer for that. She thumbed at the hammer of the shotgun as if debating whether to try a shot in such a crowd. No doubt stray pellets would strike innocent bystanders. But maybe, Odus figured, none of them were innocent. After all, they belonged to Solom, and Solom had slaughtered the Horseback Preacher.

Maybe the years had led to this moment just as surely as the Horseback Preacher's route brought him back again and again. While the past drew only farther in the distance, the Horseback Preacher was caught in an endless loop, playing out his fate with no hope of rest.

Odus was surprised to hear his own voice, not aware his thoughts slipped to his tongue. "We're here because we have to be."

"That's the same reason I'm here, Mr. Odus Dell Hampton. Because you all need me."

Odus felt the Horseback Preacher was looking straight through him, and he was sure everybody in the crowd shared the same feeling. Though the headlights must have been burning his eyes, Harmon Smith didn't squint as he surveyed the creatures gathered on the ridge.

"Let's kill the fucker," the Eakins boy said.

The Sheriff's deputy barked in an authoritative manner. "Hold it right there. Nobody gets killed here unless I say so."

Odus wondered if anyone was going to point out the irony of killing a dead man, but the assembly merely waited with half-held breath. Amos Clayton raised his shotgun but it was pointed toward the leering moon above. Will Absher, who had once been Odus's fishing buddy before Odus caught him stealing change out of his truck ashtray, stepped from the laurel thicket carrying a muzzle-loading rifle that appeared to date to back before the Civil War.

Odus wondered if that was the proper means of sending the Horseback Preacher on to heaven or hell or lands in between: a weapon from Harmon Smith's own mortal time. Odus was getting a headache from thinking over the possibilities, and decided his original idea was the best one. The way would be shown when the time was right.

If the time was right, Odus amended. He'd seen no sign that Harmon Smith was bound to die again tonight.

Sister Mary's flank muscles quivered beneath Odus, and for a moment Odus wasn't sure whether it was his own shivering, building until it was transmitted into the horse's mottled flesh.

Another handful of people leaked from the woods. As James Greene walked into the clearing leading a mule, the Horseback Preacher issued his black grin.

"One more lost child," the preacher said. "You can come out now."

CHAPTER FORTY-THREE

"Holy fucking *frijoles*," Jett said. "Some of those are *our* goats. I would recognize them anywhere, especially after they tried to munch me. See that big one, up at the front? With the brown tail? That's Dirty Harry."

A figure moved from the edge of the woods, and the crowd parted to let it through. Katy recognized the battered straw hat and the feed-sack face and fear squeezed her heart. "It's the Smith scarecrow," she whispered.

"*They always come back*," Rebecca said from nowhere. "*All of Harmon Smith's victims.*"

The scarecrow figure held a wicked-looking sickle. Its clothes were torn and rumpled, and straw leaked from the folds with each step of cracked and flapping boots. It didn't quite look human, and its limbs were too long and boneless for a man to be inside the clothing. Katy wasn't sure whether she should be relieved that Gordon wasn't wearing the costume or disturbed that the Scarecrow Man was now animated, a legend come to life.

"Told you we should have burned that piece of shit. But maybe it's not too late."

Jett unsnapped her seatbelt and was out of the car before Katy could grab her arm. "Come back here, Jett!"

But Jett was already dashing past Sue's Jeep, reaching the outer circle of goats.

"Damn," Katy grunted, getting out of the car.

"You almost killed my dad!" Jett screamed, pointing at the scarecrow, which was approaching the Horseback Preacher from the opposite side of the clearing.

The Horseback Preacher's pale and waxen face turned from Jett to the scarecrow. The grin froze on the preacher's lips. Katy pushed past Odus Hampton and Sarah Jeffers, noting the shotgun in the old woman's arms.

The goats stirred for the first time since their arrival, snorting and bleating as the scarecrow stomped into their midst. The scruffy figure stopped before the preacher and hung there as if from an invisible wire, barely touching the dirt.

"You came back," the Horseback Preacher said to the scarecrow.

The scarecrow's stitched lips gave the illusion of a wicked smile, but surely that was illusion, because the feed-sack face bore no other expression. The scarecrow hopped over a fat nanny, catching one dusty boot on a curled horn. It regained its balance and leaped—*floated,* Katy's mind screamed—onto the stone beside the Horseback Preacher.

"*Solom doesn't need you anymore,*" the scarecrow said, in a muffled and rough voice that sounded like it had been ground out of millstone. "*We can appease God ourselves.*"

"Solom needs me," the Horseback Preacher said. "Who else can bring the rain and the frost and the wind and the sun? Who else can reap the harvest in the proper season?"

The scarecrow jabbed a gloved finger at the preacher. "*You're not the only one who understands the power of blood sacrifice. You've been away too long. The old ways are worthless and Solom needs new ways. The flock is mine now.*"

Jett drew to a stop among the goats, about ten feet from the stone stage. Katy dodged around the goats, ignoring their sinister eyes and wicked teeth. Her daughter was more important to her than the whole world, and she was nearly oblivious to the strange assembly of people, many of whom held weapons and were closing in around them, tension thickening in the air like a gathering storm.

Katy sensed more than saw the movement around her: the Sheriff's deputy reaching in the car and triggering the blue strobes on the car's roof; Claude Tester dashing through the goats like a drunk running an obstacle course, rousing some to their feet as he thumped against them; their reclusive neighbor, Alex Eakins, raising what looked like a bow and aiming an arrow toward the stage.

"*Come now, my flock,*" the scarecrow said, his straw hat bouncing with his shouts. "*Accept my offering and then you shall feed.*"

A large old goat that was the spitting image of Abraham, the one that Katy had killed with her car last year, rose and stomped toward the Horseback Preacher like a repentant sinner headed for the touch of a faith healer. Other goats stood and followed.

Sarah Jeffers moved closer into shotgun range with the careful steps of the elderly. Odus whacked the paint pony on the flank and urged it toward the granite slab. Other people stirred and drew closer, wanting to be part of the malevolent miracle, some stretching out their hands like New Testament lepers reaching for the robes of Jesus.

Katy reached Jett just as the scarecrow joined the Horseback Preacher as if wanting to hog half the spotlight.

"*These are my people now,*" the scarecrow said, and Katy now recognized the cruel, commanding tone.

The Scarecrow Man—*Gordon's ghost,* she reminded herself—stood a half a foot taller than the Horseback Preacher, the brims of their hats nearly touching.

"*Have you people had enough of this preacher's ways?*" the scarecrow shouted, the stitched lips moving against the burlap face in a grotesque parody of language. "*Isn't it time we killed him once and for all, so he can gallop on back to hell?"*

"Step aside and give me a clear shot," Alex Eakins yelled back.

Claude Tester tripped over a billy goat, and the goat snapped at his flesh, teeth sinking into his arm and eliciting a scream. Claude swung the heavy wrench he was carrying as if it were David's jawbone of an ass wielded against Philistines. The scent of blood seemed to arouse the other goats, because several of them broke out of their languid stupor and sniffed the night air.

Katy looked down at the goats around her legs, relieved that their attention was still fixed on the Horseback Preacher. The goats around Jett twitched their tails but were otherwise docile.

Claude regained his balance and continued toward the stage, holding his arm, blood trickling between his fingers, the bloody wrench clutched in one fist.

Throughout all the chaos, the Horseback Preacher stood with his grave-seasoned hands at his sides, his face calm, his eyes burning like orange and red coals being fanned to life by an inner wind.

"*What has this preacher ever done for you?*" the scarecrow/Gordon-thing called to the crowd.

"Killed us, that's what," shouted Kim Deister. "And we're sick and tired of it."

Katy reached Jett and tried to pull her back, but Jett stood transfixed. Though it was difficult to tell where the burnt eyeholes of the scarecrow mask were focused, Katy felt burned by his stare, which was brighter and hotter than the beams of the collective headlights. Katy could have sworn the black yarn of lips arched into a sneer.

If Gordon's spirit was in there somewhere, he no doubt harbored a special hatred for the wife who'd betrayed him.

"Ah, my sweet little scapegoats," the scarecrow said to Katy and Jett. *"Come to offer yourself to the old gods? Come to give yourself to the soil so that Solom may be fruitful and multiply? You thwarted me last year, but maybe now you have accepted your place?"*

The scarecrow put a hand on the Horseback Preacher's shoulders and forced him to his knees. The preacher stooped so that his black hat covered his face, submitting to the scarecrow.

The scarecrow raised its voice to the crowd. *"Solom killed him a hundred and fifty years ago, but he didn't learn his lesson. He's not wanted here."*

Claude scrabbled the final few feet to the granite slab, pushing past complaining goats. "Take *me*," Claude said. "I'm the chosen one."

"No," Odus said, guiding his horse among the capricious herd. "This is my mission."

"Get off that horse and come back here," Sarah called to him. "I can't get a good shot with your big butt in the way."

To Katy, the old woman sounded almost grateful to have an excuse not to fire. Any of them could have attacked the Horseback Preacher if that was their intention. He was exposed on the rock, presumably blinded by the glaring lights, unless his vision was guided by unnatural laws.

Those at his back wouldn't have to worry about being seen and marked by whatever wrath he might unleash. It was as if the people, like the goats, were under some sort of spell, transfixed despite their hatred of the entity that brought such pain and suffering to their community.

Or maybe they were more frightened of the Scarecrow Man than the Horseback Preacher. *Better the devil you know.*

"See?" the scarecrow said, towering over the Horseback Preacher. *"Look how frail, this pathetic creature of the cloth. Look at*

the thing that has kept you cowering in your beds at night."

The scarecrow reached down a gloved hand and yanked off the preacher's hat, exposing the wiry gray hairs that curled over the pale, crenulated skull. The scarecrow sailed the hat into the herd of goats, where it caught on the horn of one and hung as if tossed atop a coat rack.

"Look upon his wonder and be disillusioned," the scarecrow shouted, his voice echoing off the granite boulders. *"Know him by his fruits."*

Katy wanted to drag Jett back to the Subaru but found herself as rapt and awestruck as the rest. This close to the drama, she detected not only the electric aura of the Horseback Preacher, but the scarecrow's corrupt radiance as well. She couldn't deny the magnetism of his authority.

"What's he doing and why doesn't that policeman stop him?" Jett whispered.

"Because the policeman's human," Katy said. "Like the rest of us."

"Gordon needs to die for real."

"That's not Gordon, honey."

"Like hell. See what an asshole he is?"

The scarecrow slammed the preacher facedown against the stone and planted a scuffed boot on his back, grinding the heel into the preacher's yielding flesh.

Claude tried to climb up onto the stone slab. It was slick with dew, and his wounded arm prevented him from gaining solid purchase in the crevices. He lodged one boot into a crack and was about to haul himself up onto the impromptu stage when one of the goats in the front row, whose brown facial fur made a raccoon mask, lurched forward and snagged his other leg, tugging on the cuff of his jeans.

Another goat, this one with crooked beige horns, pushed forward and began sniffing his calf. "Help me," Claude called.

A hissing *thwack* pierced a hole in the night, and the goat with the beige horns let out a bruised bleat of shock. The feathers of an arrow tip jutted from its rib cage, just above its heart. It staggered back two steps, wobbled, and collapsed as if its legs were pipe cleaners.

"*No!*" the scarecrow moaned, as though the injury had been inflicted on it instead of the goat—as if they were connected somehow.

"The fucker munched my stash, man," Alex said. "That was private property. *My* property."

The goats near the one that had fallen began sniffing the warm corpse. One poked out a tentative tongue and licked the wound. The herd began bleating and lowing, giving off restless snorts, more of them rising on their knobby legs.

"Come on, Jett," Katy said. "We've got to get out of here."

A grizzled billy goat, one eye made milky by blindness, nipped the air a couple of inches from Katy's leg, brown teeth clacking with menace. She eyed the distance back to the Subaru. The rock slab was closer, but that would put them within the scarecrow's reach. The scarecrow pointed his sickle at Alex, his boot still pressing on the preacher's back.

Words issued from behind the scarecrow's mask: "*You should forgive those who trespass against you.*"

"Maybe you should take better care of your fences," Alex said, notching another arrow.

CHAPTER FORTY-FOUR

Sarah didn't quite mean to squeeze the trigger.

At least, that's what she told herself. But an old woman's reflexes, like all her physical responses, tended to decline with every go-round of the sun. The recoil nearly knocked her to the ground, but she wobbled back into balance.

The echo of the gun's report slapped off the granite boulders and rolled through the trees. Blue-gray smoke swirled in the Jeep's headlights, and the strong bite of cordite drowned out the moist humus smell of the mountain and the stench of the goats. The frail bones of her shoulder ached from the gun's kick.

She'd meant to take down those goats nearest to Claude, because they looked ready to chomp down on his legs. But what really flipped her was spying the goat that raided her store. She didn't usually carry a grudge, and believed all God's creature's had a rightful place in the world. But this was the same world that held monsters like the Horseback Preacher and that scarecrow thing.

In that frozen moment, Sarah had time to absorb tiny details just as the night exploded: Sue Norwood opening the driver's-side door of the Jeep; Odus sitting tall on the bareback horse and looking around like a rustler wondering where to direct the stampede; Alex Eakins taking aim at either the scarecrow or the Horseback Preacher; Claude scrambling onto the flat slab of stone.

Sarah broke down the barrel and thumbed out the warm, spent shell, reaching in her blouse pocket for a fresh round.

+++

Katy sensed the change in the animals after one of their number had fallen.

The night was charged with rage and confusion. Katy heard the soft *snick* of an arrow as it penetrated the scarecrow's straw-stuffed chest. The arrow passed almost completely through the thing's body, with only the feathers protruding. The supernatural creature reached behind its back, found the tip of the arrow, and pulled it the rest of the way through.

It laughed—*just like Gordon*, Katy thought—and flung the arrow against the stone. "*Only the dead can kill the dead*," the scarecrow shouted with profane glee. "*But the dead can kill the living, too.*"

Maybe that was what Rebecca had been trying to tell Katy, but then, why did the ghost guide them up the mountain to this madness in the first place?

"*Fetch him!*" the scarecrow yelled, waving his sickle at Alex. At first Katy thought he was addressing the crowd, but the goats turned as one and sniffed the air in Alex's direction. The goats gave out cries and squeaks as they moved. Alex backed away as the goats nearest him broke into a trot. There was no way he'd make the relative safety of the woods. Even if he did, the sure-footed goats would have an advantage on the rough terrain.

The horn of a passing goat grazed Katy's wrist, laying open the skin.

"Shit, Mom, you're bleeding," Jett said.

Jett wasn't the only one who noticed. A long-bearded nanny paused, bucking against the river of goats and turning toward Katy. It sniffed, snorted, and kicked up its back legs, clicking its hooves. Then it struggled against the seething tide of animals and headed for Katy as if she'd been dipped in honey and oats.

"The rock," Katy said, gripping Jett's hand so hard her own fingers ached. "Climb."

The nanny negotiated the rumbling herd better than Katy did, because she was busy dodging bobbing horns and stomping hooves. The nanny was gaining, and Katy was still twenty feet from the rock. And even if she reached the rock, what would the scarecrow do to her? Cut her with his sickle, or toss her to the meat-eating monsters that somehow obeyed his perverted commands?

The decision was taken from her as a passing goat rammed her in the stomach, knocking the wind from her. Above the high-pitched whining in her ears, she heard Jett scream, and a hundred hoof beats drummed their death march. Then she was lifted into the air, yanked as if by the ray of a flying saucer or the crook of God's swooping shepherd's staff. She blinked the lime-colored sparks of pain from behind her eyes and found herself flopped belly-down over the back of Odus's horse.

"Where's Jett?" she managed to whisper, breath like wet cement in her lungs.

"Can't reach her," Odus said. He slapped the horse on the thigh and said, "Come on, Sister Mary, let's ride out this stampede."

The horse whinnied and reared, jostling Katy, and for a horrifying split-second she thought she would be hurled from the horse and back among the milling goats. But she grabbed the horse's neck and held on as they waded through the herd, which was thinning now as the stragglers made their way toward Alex.

Another shotgun blast sounded, and two goats bleated

squeals of pain. Katy saw Jett at the edge of the rock, climbing up, finding handholds on the mossy surface, gaining her footing.

The scarecrow released the Horseback Preacher, grabbed Jett by the hair, and yanked her against his ragged clothing. *"You're mine,"* the creepy Gordon-voice said.

Jett managed to kick free before the sickle could descend, and the Horseback Preacher rolled over and rammed into the scarecrow's spindly legs. As they grappled, Jett fled to the edge of the flat boulder, but the turbulent ocean of lethal goats prevented her from jumping to the ground.

"We have to save her," Katy shouted in Odus's ear so she could be heard over the bleating and panicky cries.

"These goats have gone crazy," Odus said. "Look. They're *eating* people."

He was right. Alex reached a beech tree and scrambled up into the safety of the branches. Two goats butted the tree trunk, but its girth was several feet in diameter and the tree barely shook. A man screamed as another shot rang out, and Katy looked around to see the deputy with a goat latched onto his leg, another biting the hand that held his pistol. A wounded goat shivered at the officer's feet, thrown into spasms by a head wound.

Kim Deister got off a burst of gunfire that felled several of the creatures, but then she was dragged under a snapping, snarling horde of them. One ragged red hand reached out of the chaos, quivered, and then fell limp.

Sarah Jeffers dropped her shotgun and climbed onto the hood of the Jeep, and several goats tried to clamber up the bumper. An old man in a leather jacket, whom Katy didn't recognize, leveled his shotgun and blasted toward the Jeep, sending pellets scattering across the metal and driving the goats away. The old woman cursed and gripped her knee.

A woman and a younger man with pitchforks stood back-to-back, jabbing at the goats that encircled them.

"All hell's breaking loose," Katy said.

"We were already in hell," Odus said. "We've gone way past that now."

"I've got to reach Jett," Katy said.

"Best to get away from here or we're all dead."

The goats lost their communal goal and scattered into the night, chasing the people who had been summoned to the surreal revival. Their bleats became guttural cries of hunger. Katy saw one digging its teeth into the neck of one of its brethren that had fallen victim to a gunshot.

Odus guided Sister Mary toward the logging road, urging the horse into a trot. But Katy kicked free, falling to the ground, twisting her ankle as she rolled. She struggled to her feet in the rough, tilled soil where the goats romped. Goat manure streaked the knees of her pants, and the smell was enough to make her vomit.

But she blocked that out, along with the screams of the people and the unnerving cries of the goats. She focused on the rock, where the eerie scarecrow grappled with the preacher, two nightmares in a bizarre battle *royale*.

Katy limped toward Jett, stepping over the preacher's trampled hat. A goat trotted past her, a dripping chunk of what looked like potted meat clamped between its buck teeth.

Jett crawled around the rock's edge toward Katy, reaching to help her up.

The scarecrow drove its sickle in a swift arc and dragged its tip across the preacher's back, slicing into the black wool coat and causing a gush of milky fluid to erupt from the preacher's flesh. The scarecrow spun, shaking liquid from the wet sickle, and grabbed Jett with one gloved hand.

He yanked her upright and into a scratchy embrace and let

the sickle slide lower.

CHAPTER FORTY-FIVE

The buck-toothed bastards had him treed like a raccoon.

Alex dropped his Pearson bow when the herd started chasing him. He'd managed one decent shot at Weird Dude, but that scarecrow fucker had gotten in the way. And the arrow to the heart hadn't even slowed it down. The government must have cooked up some serious mutant shit with that particular project, no doubt wasting ten billion tax dollars in the process.

He looked down at the bleating, sneering creature closest to him, who was reared up on the tree trunk. The strange eyes with their boxy, oblate pupils glittered in the gloomy sweep of headlights.

"Yeah, you'd eat the original U.S. Constitution if it was right there in front of you, wouldn't you?" he taunted. "The powderheads wrote it on hemp paper, and I know how much you bastards love hemp."

The goat twitched its ears in fury, and another goat butted the tree, horns clacking against the bark.

Alex wasn't in position to work the submachine gun, but he unfastened the snap on his hip holster and drew out the Colt Python. Weird Dude and the scarecrow were still on the rock and out of pistol range, so he couldn't take down their shepherd.

But the goats seemed to be over their Weird Dude trip and now acted like they worked for the scarecrow fucker. And the scarecrow was holding the neighbor Goth girl. A man's private business was a man's private business, but it didn't look like your typical Hallmark Family Special moment.

Alex aimed the pistol down in a two-handed grip. The goat stared back along the length of the barrel.

"You are one fuggly piece of work." Alex squeezed the trigger and a brown dot erupted on the animal's forehead. He knew goats possessed thick skulls because of their bizarre mating rituals that sometimes caused them to butt heads until one of the males dropped from exhaustion. They weren't symbols of depraved lust for nothing.

But a Python bullet was more than a match for the thick plate of bone, though the entry wound was a little messier than usual. The back of the goat's head exploded, raining bits of meat and bone on the half-dozen goats surrounding the base of the tree.

The goat's lips peeled back in a grin.

Leave it to the government to build a goat that wouldn't die.

THE NARROW GATE 253

CHAPTER FORTY-SIX

Jett squirmed in the Scarecrow Man's grip, nearly sneezing from the dusty, moldy stench of him.

Her throat hurt where he stuck the point of his sickle against her skin, and a warm trickle descended the slope of her neck. The persistent strobe of the police lights made her dizzy as screams and frantic bleats blended into a muddy music. Gunshots thundered here and there across the woods as people fought off the attacking goats.

She met her mom's eyes and could read the look. That sappy old "We'll get through this together," but for the first time, Jett welcomed it and *needed* it.

Whatever this scarecrow was—a demon, Gordon's ghost, or something conjured by the Horseback Preacher—it was as solid and real as the stone beneath her. And the sickle was real, its blade cold and sharp.

The burlap face rasped her cheek as she struggled, and the burnt eyeholes in the mask revealed two hellish sparks of light, as if some mad fire burned away inside. He squeezed the breath from her and hooked the sickle around her neck. One upward jerk of the blade and she'd be as headless as Rebecca.

Katy scrambled atop the rock. "Let her go, Gordon. If you need a sacrifice, take me."

"*I'm not Gordon,*" the scarecrow said. "*I'm something more.*"

Jett could barely draw air into her lungs, but she wheezed, "Run, Mom!"

Katy glanced down at the prone form of the Horseback

Preacher, and Jett knew what she was thinking: *Is he going to save us again?*

But it looked like the Gordon/scarecrow thing had won the turf war and now was ready to pillage.

"*I'll accept your sacrifice,*" the scarecrow said to Katy. "*But I'm taking this little bitch, too. All of you belong to me now.*"

Jett was going to die here with all these outlandish characters and be stuck in the afterlife asylum of Solom forever. Her only hope was that Mom would keep her promise of getting through it together, but she didn't see an exit from this one.

Katy took another step forward as a bullet glanced off the stone between her feet, kicking up a spark. A staccato burst of gunfire strafed the Horseback Preacher, but his limp form didn't move as the bullets tore through the dark cloth of his suit.

Dead for good this time.

"If you kill us, I'm going to haunt your ass until hell turns into a skating rink," Katy said to the scarecrow.

It chuffed with laughter, bits of straw flying out from between the stitched lips and spraying Jett's cheek.

CHAPTER FORTY-SEVEN

Alex had used up the rounds in the Colt Python, but the goats still circled below him.

A couple had fallen, those whose limbs were clipped by bullets, but none of them died, despite shots that landed between the eyes or dead-on in the heart. Sure, the wounds slowed them down a little, but it also made them angrier, like a hive of bees that had been kicked. The marijuana they'd munched must have made them ornery instead of mellowing them out.

Alex adjusted his position in the branches and fumbled the AKR submachine gun into his lap. He kicked back the lever and surveyed the clearing. Weird Dude Walking and the scarecrow creep had been going at it like a Republican and a Democrat fighting over a defense contract, but now Weird Dude appeared down for the count. The scarecrow cradled the neighbor girl, the Goth with the black bangs, in his grip and Alex couldn't risk a shot from this distance. The Smith widow stood with them, helpless as the goats churned and bucked around them.

He glanced around to see how the others were faring.

The handyman, Odus, was squaring off with another figure on a horse, like knights preparing for a joust. The gloaming cast by the headlights must have messed with his vision, because he could have sworn the figure astride the big bay horse had no head.

+++

Odus was skirting the groups of goats, looking for a route through them to the flat boulder where Katy and Jett were trapped.

The Scarecrow Man's appearance had been a shock, but he'd considered the Horseback Preacher the true threat. Now, he wasn't so sure if trusting Providence to deliver his instrument of conquest was such a smart move.

But when he spied Rebecca's headless corpse astride Old Saint, galloping hell-bent for leather toward the boulder, he figured she was taking the horse to the preacher. And once mounted, old Harmon might just become too powerful for all of them to deal with, no matter how many guns they brought to bear.

Better head her off at the pass.

Odus couldn't tell if he'd guided Sister Mary or if the horse propelled itself through some inner command. Either way, the paint pony offered enough giddy-up to break both their necks. As the distance narrowed, he got a good look at the thing riding Old Saint. He'd worked for the Smiths before Rebecca had been killed and always thought her the sweetest of ladies. Plus she cooked up a mean parsnip pie.

But now she looked to be serving up a different kind of meanness, one brought on by the anger of the grave. She seemed barely there, her head fading in and out, her cotton-shift body nearly see-through in the moonlight. But Old Saint looked massive and solid, a stud with rippling muscles and strong flanks. Twice the weight of Sister Mary, the horse was liable to knock them into next week, skipping Sunday on the way.

Odus was close enough to see the steamy breath pluming from Old Saint's nostrils. Then Rebecca's head materialized, her eyes like dark holes that ate everything that entered them, long hair fluttering out behind her. The gap in her neck flapped like a second screaming mouth.

He kicked his heels against Sister Mary's ribs, but she was already at top speed, juddering his bones in their sockets as they thundered toward the unknown.

+++

Bullets flew and the people of Solom screamed.

Sue clambered onto the hood of the Jeep, the pick-ax in her fist. Hearing the *thrump* of metal, the goats turned again and leaped up onto the vehicle, trying to get a foothold on the dew-slick front bumper.

"About time you came to the rescue," Sarah said. "I thought I'd hooked up with the wrong spunky sidekick for a second there."

"I haven't rescued either of us yet," she said, digging the point of the pick-ax into the Jeep's soft-top.

A goat gained enough traction to leap forward and nip her shoe. Sarah stomped on the animal's head, bouncing it like a coconut and with about as much effect. Sue peeled a long gap into the canvas top.

"Climb in," she said, and as she helped Sarah work her knobby limbs over the windshield and into the Jeep, a twin shriek of whinnies slit the night.

+++

The scarecrow was so fascinated by the showdown between the horses that he seemed to forget Jett was there.

Katy lunged for the sickle, jamming her hand between the blade and Jett's flesh. If the Gordon/scarecrow sliced now, he'd take her fingers, but Jett might have a chance.

Fourteen hundred pounds of horse flesh collided and the forest shuddered.

For one long second, the animals merged, Rebecca's head flying away from the impact. The spotted horse and the giant black horse were a tangle of knotted knees, forelegs, hooves, and stringy hair. They appeared to be one quivering mass of gristle and meat, stirred into a living soup.

Rebecca's rickety rack of skin and the dry bone that wore her features became part of the orgiastic wad of insane magic, but Odus was thrown clear and rolled to a pained heap in the grass.

Katy forced herself to look away, despite the odd energy that crackled around the showdown. She tugged on the scarecrow's glove and it slid a few inches away from the ragged shirt sleeve, straw spilling to the ground.

Stuffing. Nothing but stuffing.

There's no Gordon in here.

Then the burlap face turned to look at her, the stitched lips stretching into a smile, and she realized she was wrong.

CHAPTER FORTY-EIGHT

The scarecrow's grip loosened as Katy clawed at the sickle, and Jett shifted and shoved against the nightmare creature.

Jett heard thundering hooves and thought a goat was charging. She looked away from the stone stage to see Rebecca mounted on a horse and galloping toward them.

She wore her scarecrow garb, the effigy they'd left in the back seat of the Subaru, and the white linen flowed out behind her like a burial shroud.

The monstrous horse grew more solid, his hooves hammering sixty feet away, then fifty, clumps of dirt flying in his wake. But it wasn't just a horse—it was a roiling, suppurating mass with too many legs and a wild mane that trailed behind it more than ten feet.

"*Gordon!*" came Rebecca's voice, and it was a voice that didn't need a mouth—it seemed to pour from the gash in her neck as if forced up from the blackest depths of hell's deepest well.

"I'm not Gordon anymore," the scarecrow bellowed. "*You're as stupid dead as you were before I killed you.*"

Jett realized Katy was pulling at the scarecrow's glove, and Jett understood. She felt weird doing it, but she drove her hand into the gap just above the thing's jeans, in the gap where the plain shirt met the waistband. She clutched a fistful of straw and raked it out, and the scarecrow roared in either pain or rage.

"*I still belong to you,*" Rebecca howled, her words rising about the frenzied bleating of goats around them. "*After all, I was your first."*

Then Rebecca gripped the horse's mane in her fists and tugged, urging the animal to leap onto the boulder. Jett barely had time to grab one more fistful of the scarecrow's innards before Katy pulled her away.

Gordon tried to swing the sickle—either at Jett and Katy, the monster horse, or Rebecca, or maybe all three at once—but the weapon tumbled away, the glove still attached to it.

The horse slammed into the scarecrow, busting the plaid shirt at the seams and sending straw cascading to the ground. The horse stomped and kicked, a hoof mashing the burlap face into a lumpy mess and shredding the straw hat.

Katy hugged Jett and they rolled off the stone into the wet grass. Goat hooves padded around them, and Jett thought for sure they were going to get munched, but the animals tottered past them.

As they got to their feet, they discovered the goats had found a tastier treat: the scarecrow man.

As Rebecca dismounted, the horse-creature dipped its long snout and sniffed at the straw, then pulled a bit of it between its broad, blunt teeth and began chewing, too.

+++

"Did you see that?" Sarah asked Sue.

"No, and neither did you. I don't want to spend the rest of my days in the nuthouse."

"You ain't crazy. I guess you've just been officially welcomed to Solom."

Sue brought the Jeep to a halt beside Odus, who was woozy but appeared to be in no danger of sudden death. Unless one of those stray bullets caught him. Sarah opened the door and crawled into the back, leaving room for Odus to crawl into the Jeep.

"Where's my horse?" Odus said, as groggy as if he were on a two-pint drunk.

"I think it headed for greener pastures," Sarah said.

+++

The goats grazed sedately.

The ones that were outside the pack eating the scarecrow's straw were content to work the lush autumn grass of the clearing. The dew sparkled under the moon, and the dark bullet wounds in their hides glistened like eyes. The tableau was strangely beautiful, and Katy was sure she'd never see anything so mysterious again.

She wasn't even sure she'd seen it the first time.

"You okay?" she asked Jett, kissing her daughter's forehead.

"I...think so. Rebecca?"

"Gone like smoke," Katy said.

"She got her revenge."

"Only the dead can kill the dead."

They picked their way through the remaining goats to check on Odus, Sue, and Sarah. Several corpses lay in the clearing, ravaged by bite marks. The bar light atop the deputy's car still threw its strobing blue wash across the night.

When they reached the Jeep, Odus said, "You guys okay?"

"A few scrapes and bruises, but we're still breathing," Katy said. "As if that makes much difference in Solom."

"Where's the Horseback Preacher?" Sarah asked in a weary, old-woman voice.

Katy glanced back at the boulder, assuming he'd been eaten by the animals as well, but not a scrap of black wool remained. "I didn't see him."

"Me, neither," Jett said. "I was kind of occupied there, trying not to get my head cut off."

"I hope to God Rebecca took him down," Odus said. "Two birds with one stone."

"We figured the goats were the Horseback Preacher's, but we were wrong," Sarah said. "They were marching for that scarecrow."

"Maybe so, but I'm not taking any chances." Sue started the Jeep. "I'm getting out of here while they're still occupied."

"Wait," Katy said. "What about these casualties? What about the police and the rescue squad?"

"Solom," Odus said.

Katy nodded. She wondered how many times such surreal showdowns had taken place over the years here. She'd never be able to give a rational explanation for what had happened tonight. That one word "Solom" seemed as good a reason as any.

Other vehicle engines roared to life in the night, as if all the people awoke from their nightmares and were ready to return to their sleepless dreams in the valley below. The Jeep jerked forward and headed for the logging road, other vehicles already lining up to head back down the mountain.

"Let's go home," Katy said, throwing an exhausted arm over Jett's shoulders.

"Wait a second," Jett said. She took off jogging across the grass.

Alarmed, Katy glanced around, wondering if some new threat was afoot. She saw only their reclusive neighbor, Alex Eakins, who emerged from the dark forest and waved. Some sort of gun dangled from a strap around his neck.

"Hello, Mrs. Smith," he called.

"Logan," she said. "I never took Gordon's name."

"Guess you're glad of that now."

"I'm just glad to be alive." She watched Jett bend over and pick up something, hoping it wasn't a body part or some sort of talisman that would end up cursing them until the end of time.

"The government put on quite a show this time," Alex said.

"What's that?"

"You know. Secret genetic experiments, bullshit Black Ops maneuvers conducted in the name of national security." He pulled out a cigarette, stuffed it in his mouth, and sparked a lighter. When he touched the flame to its tip, she smelled the smoke.

"Is that marijuana?" she asked.

He exhaled. "Live free or die."

"Could you please…my daughter…she's…"

"Oh," he said. "Right. Morals and shit."

He tossed the joint to the ground and rubbed it out with his boot. "Well, I better get to work. Plenty of firewood around here, and I figure Lost Ridge could use a controlled burn. If I do the government's job for them, maybe the cover-up will slide on by without dragging us into it too much."

"You're going to start a forest fire?"

He grinned. "You won't finger me, will you?"

"Good neighbors mind their own business."

"You got that right,' he said, turning and heading back to the woods.

"Who was that?" Jett asked, rejoining her mother. She held something round in her hands the size of a small basketball.

"A freedom fighter, I think. What have you got?"

Jett held up the head of the female scarecrow. "I figured we should put this with the rest of her. She'll probably sleep easier that way."

So will we, Katy thought.

CHAPTER FORTY-NINE

Arvel Ward opened his cellar door.

He'd spent a sleepless night downstairs, the bare bulb burning, the air ripe from the earthen floor's odor, jars of jelly and pickled okra lining the shelves. As morning's first gray light leaked through the narrow, high-set windows, the warmth of joy replaced the autumnal chill in his heart.

He'd survived.

The Horseback Preacher may have walked up the stairs and taken Betsy, just as the preacher had taken his brother Zeke all those years ago, but Arvel made it. Arvel was safe until the next round of the circuit, and with any luck and by the grace of God he'd find a natural grave before then. There was comfort in the sleep of dirt and worms, but until then he would get along as best he could, living right and keeping his tools clean.

Arvel went into the living room. The air smelled of damp smoke, which was odd because they'd burned no fire in the hearth last night.

When he'd gone into hiding, he'd forgotten his chewing tobacco, and the ache was on him strong. He opened the foil pouch with trembling fingers and stuffed a wad of shredded leaves inside his cheek. The nicotine bit sweet and hard.

He almost swallowed the wad when he turned and saw the Horseback Preacher sitting on the couch. Betsy had draped an oversize knitted doily over the back of it, and somehow the preacher seemed even more of an intrusion, sitting there among the tidy pillows.

"Not expecting company?" the Horseback Preacher said, thumbing the wide brim of his black hat. The preacher smelled of spoiled meat and rotted cloth, and his fingernails were dark with dirt, as if he'd clawed his way up from the grave.

Up close, Arvel could see the holes in the Horseback Preacher's wool suit. There was no flesh behind them, only an emptiness that stretched as long as every nightmare tunnel ever traveled.

Arvel spat out the tobacco, but his involuntary swallow sent a slug's length of bitter juice down his throat.

"It ain't my turn," Arvel whined. "Tuh-take Betsy. She's upstairs, helpless as a cut kitten, and she ain't going to put up much of a struggle."

"Neither will you."

"I didn't mean to lie to you that one time," Arvel blubbered. "I was just a boy."

"You said you knew where to find my horse. But I found him without your help."

Arvel backed away, wondering if he could reach the fireplace poker and if the steel bar would do any good against a creature that seemed to be built of *nothing*. "You can't take me," Arvel said, nearly giggling in relief. "The sun done come up."

The Horseback Preacher stood, tall and gangly. "I don't make the rules, Arvel," he said, adjusting his hat. "I only serve them."

"Buh-buh-but you've already claimed a soul for this trip around."

"I've claimed nothing yet. Solom has."

"It ain't my *turrrrn*." The tears were hot and wet on his cheeks, the living room blurred, and Arvel took in the familiar surroundings of his house, a place that he knew he'd never see again. At least, not from *this* side of the border between dead and alive.

"Hush, now, or you'll wake Betsy. She needs her rest." The Horseback Preacher gave a tired, benevolent smile and reached his long, waxy fingers toward Arvel.

CHAPTER FIFTY

Harmon Smith unhitched Old Saint from the lilac bush.

The horse was a little different, more robust somehow, as if a few of the years had been rolled back. A little rejuvenation by means of sacrifice seemed to do him good.

Harmon considered letting the horse munch on the fading, frost-browned flower bed a little longer, but Betsy had suffered enough already. She'd need the busy work to distract her from the loss of her husband, whose body lay cooling on the kitchen floor, near where the goat attacked Betsy.

If the authorities were summoned once they cleaned up the mess on Lost Ridge, they might rule it a heart attack, or they might say it was an accidental fall. Most likely, they'd say, "Solom."

Calling them "authorities" was a silly, mortal concept anyway. Only one authority existed, and Its hand set the wheel in motion. But such things didn't trouble the Horseback Preacher. His duty was given, and he was a good servant.

Something whimpered underneath the porch. Harmon knelt and peered into the darkness. "Here, Digger. It's all okay now."

The dog hauled itself out, whining. Harmon patted its flanked. "Good boy. Thanks for keeping quiet when I got here. There's food inside if you want. Door's open."

Digger glanced up into the preacher's face, licked his lips with a swipe of pink tongue, and gave an enthusiastic bark.

"Hush, now. Betsy needs her rest."

Digger sat on his haunches and sniffed the air. Harmon

gazed thoughtfully over at the Smith farm, but all he could see was the top of the barn. He wasn't one for sentiment, but blood was blood, after all, and the Smiths had owned the land for centuries. One day he might have to drop in again, just for old time's sake.

The Horseback Preacher hauled himself up into the familiar cup of Old Saint's saddle. He gazed at the rim of Lost Ridge, where black smoke boiled against the red morning sky. Hell would have been proud of such scenery.

"Come on, Saint, we've got places to be," he said, giving a gentle lift to the reins. He didn't have to point toward a destination. The horse, fat on souls and shrubs, knew the route as intimately as Harmon did.

Narrow is the gate and hard the road that leads to life and light, truth and heaven, and there the road ends in peace for those fortunate enough to find it.

But all other routes are twisting and endless. And on these trails, the Horseback Preacher rides alone.

THE END

Scott Nicholson is the international bestselling author of more than 20 books. He lives in the Blue Ridge Mountains of North Carolina, where he tends an organic garden, strums guitar, and practices armchair Taoism.

Visit him at www.AuthorScottNicholson.com or email him at hauntedcomputerbooks@gmail.com.

OTHER BOOKS BY SCOTT NICHOLSON

Solom #1: The Scarecrow

Solom #3: The Preacher

Liquid Fear

Chronic Fear

After #1: The Shock

After #2: The Echo

After #3: Milepost 291

Disintegration

The Red Church

Drummer Boy

McFall

Kiss Me or Die

Speed Dating with the Dead

The Skull Ring

The Harvest

The Home

Creative Spirit

October Girls (as L.C. Glazebrook)

Scattered Ashes

Monster's Ink

Thank You for the Flowers

They Hunger

Bad Blood (Spider #1)

Cursed (with J.R. Rain)

Dirt

Grave Conditions